George Henry Calvert, Johann Wolfgang von Goethe

Charlotte von Stein

George Henry Calvert, Johann Wolfgang von Goethe

Charlotte von Stein

ISBN/EAN: 9783741124365

Manufactured in Europe, USA, Canada, Australia, Japa

Cover: Foto ©Andreas Hilbeck / pixelio.de

Manufactured and distributed by brebook publishing software
(www.brebook.com)

George Henry Calvert, Johann Wolfgang von Goethe

Charlotte von Stein

CHARLOTTE VON STEIN.

A Memoir.

BY

GEORGE H. CALVERT.

BOSTON:
LEE AND SHEPARD, PUBLISHERS.
NEW YORK:
CHARLES T. DILLINGHAM.
1877.

PREFACE.

In 1848–51 were first published, in Germany, by A. Schoell, in three volumes, the Letters of Goethe to Frau von Stein, from 1776 to 1826. In 1874 appeared two volumes entitled, *Charlotte von Stein, Goethe's Freundin. Ein Lebensbild, mit Benutzung der Familienpapiere entworfen von Heinrich Düntzer.* (Charlotte von Stein, Goethe's Friend; A Life-Picture, portrayed through the Means of Family Papers, by Henry Düntzer.) From these two works have been drawn the facts and letters used in writing the following volume. Slight use, also, has been made of the correspondence of Merck, and of the letters of Goethe to Lavater and to the Countess Stolberg.

The reading of the letters of Goethe to Frau von Stein, many years ago, awakened in the author a strong interest in the woman who could inspire such letters, and curiosity in regard to her was copiously gratified by the publication, three years since, of the two compact volumes of Düntzer. The personality and gifts of Charlotte von Stein, which made her a distinguished figure in an illustrious circle, make her a choice subject for biography. On becoming acquainted with the details of her long career, furnished by abundant family documents and other sources, one understands why Goethe in his early manhood was so captivated. To the writer of this volume she seemed one whose doings and sayings and influence are interesting and instructive enough to entitle them to transplantation out of their native German soil. Under this conviction the following memoir was written.

The first portrait, in front of the volume, represents Charlotte when she was about thirty years of age; the second, towards the close, when she was eighty. The castle, at the beginning of chapter II., is Kochberg.

NEWPORT, R. I., *July, 1877.*

CONTENTS.

———————

CHARLOTTE VON STEIN.

I.

CHILDHOOD.

THE marshal of the ducal household of Saxe-Weimar-Eisenach, John Christian William von Schardt, was somewhat hard by nature. A stern superior, devoted to his official routine, and believing that the main support of prosperous being is outward order, he took little account of the inward springs which make of humanity a "perpetual motion."

In the year 1742 the marshal was for a moment startled out of his thought that municipal arrangement and court etiquette were, to the Duchy of Saxe-Weimar-Eisenach, of as supreme moment as are to the earth the rising and setting of the sun. On Christmas Day of that year was laid before him his first infant, to which his young wife, thirteen years younger than himself, had just given birth.

The strange joy with which the marshal gazed
upon this new link of humanity was almost
quenched in awe. Vividly came home to him
the mystery of life and creation, mingled with
a sudden rush of responsibility that was op-
pressive. But all other feeling was soon swallowed up in parental rapture. The rigorous
marshal felt his heart soften ; and a tear almost rounded itself for a leap from his eye, as
he looked at the wonderful little creature that
owed its being to him. The babe opened its
dark eyes, — those eyes that were to grow so
large and beautiful, that for eighty-five years
were to reflect on their surface, with rare clearness, a vast variegated procession of personages and events, and at the same time in their
lucent depths embrace an interior world pal-
pitating with more than usual liveliness, a
changeful world of joys and sorrows, of triumphs and disappointments, of trials and satis-
factions.

Charlotte Albertine Ernestine was the name
given to the infant. The father of Charlotte
was of a Silesian stock ; her mother of North
British descent, kindred of old dominant fam-
ilies in Scotland. The mother was a peace-
ful, religious woman, earnest, substantial, in
whom sensibility was married to common

sense. She made no claims upon the world, and in submissive dutifulness as wife, and active dutifulness as mother, found daily compensation for the common ills of life. In dutifulness there is an inner strength that straightens man or woman against the harshest blasts that outwardness can blow, a divine liveliness, that is forever cleansing the heart and lifting it into the light of happiness, even when sorrows most press their darkness round it.

One defect of the marshal, an unconscious defect, was want of sympathy with childhood. A man of routine and of measured, calculated movement, the spontaneity of children and their lawlessness (which is obedience to a deeper law) was something to be suppressed, like their noise. He would have frowned had he been told that their noise and impetuous motion are a sign of health and growth, and a help to both. Under his roof the severity of outward regulation was happily mitigated by frequent absences from home on court duty, as well as by the silent counteraction of the mother, whose warmth and judgment took from mechanical, unsympathetic rules much of their angularity and hardness. Thus did Charlotte grow out of infancy into childhood, amid younger sisters and brothers, under influences as little unfavor-

able to the unfolding of a superior feminine
nature as on an average could be looked for in
the middle of the eighteenth century in Weimar
or Saxony, or, as for that, in any part of Christendom.

Charlotte, as her tall slender shape lifted itself out of childhood into girlhood, suffered no
such curtailment of freedom as would distort
or cramp her mental growth, while, on the
other hand, the paternal martinet,— as is apt
to be the case with the one-sided who have sap
in them, — had his serviceable side. He was
strong in the valuation of muscular development through suitable bodily exercise, and at
the same time set the highest store by the ac-
complishments and elegances that grace a
court. Charlotte had reached her fourteenth
year, when a marriage occurred which, besides
being of happy importance to her, turned out
to be the fountain-head of a clear stream that
brought refreshment and strength to the Duchy
of Weimar, and not to Weimar alone, but to all
Germany.

Early in 1756 the young sovereign duke,
Constantine, just declared of legal age on com-
pleting his eighteenth year, went a-wooing to
Brunswick, and at the end of March returned
to Weimar, bringing with him a lovely bride, a

year younger than himself, Anna Amalia, niece to the great Frederick of Prussia, — a kinship which might have been the lot of any princess; but Amalia was more than that ; she was benefactress to her husband's duchy, which not one princess in a hundred has the heavenly gifts to become.

A year after the marriage there was jubilation throughout the loyal duchy over the birth of an heir ; and about the same time Charlotte was appointed lady in waiting to the duchess. The chiefs of the court being so young, a court-lady of fifteen was in place, and Charlotte was somewhat premature in mind as in person.

Thus by a fortunate marriage was laid the foundation for Weimar's distinction and renown ; and a thoroughly good marriage, that is, a marriage where two individual halves are united to make a tolerably harmonious unit, is with princes even more a matter of luck than with their subjects. This Brunswick Princess Amalia proved herself a good mother ; and, in her case what heightened her excellence as mother, she was a great sovereign, for sovereign superiority and executive mastery are not necessarily measured by breadth of territory ruled over.

The general joy at the birth of a ducal heir

was clouded by war, that terrible war of seven
years, which had just broken out, and in which
Amalia's uncle, Frederick of Prussia, astonished
Europe and earned his title of Great. The
very day on which the welcome heir was born,
three hundred imperial troops occupied Weimar, while Frederick was hovering in the
neigborhood. A few days later, after a battle
near by, the town was again invaded by
thousands of hungry Austrians and French.
Again, after the battle of Rossbach, the flying
French and Austrians swept through the little town and duchy like an angered greedy
whirlwind.

Fearful trials were these. War-driven hosts
devour and devastate worse than pitiless armies
of locusts or grasshoppers. And the gloom
thus caused was to be still deepened in the little capital and over the whole duchy. The
young Duke Constantine fell ill, and died before
he had reached his twenty-first year. Amalia
was a widow at the age of nineteen, with an
infant heir, to whom was to be added a brother,
born three months after Constantine's death.
To her, as to the whole population, the blow
seemed crushing, irreparable. What resources
lie dormant in an individual woman of nineteen
cannot be surmised, even by herself; still less

could any tearful eye be prophetic enough to behold in the infant heir, who lay there apparently left helpless in the cold rough world, the future grand duke, Charles Augustus, the gallant warrior, the enlightened liberal sovereign, the illustrious friend of Goethe.

Men make circumstances, and thus raise the chief obstacle to their own well-being, which obstacle is the adversity of circumstances. When a new generation arrives at its place, it finds, for the most part, the circumstances in which and with which it is to work so discouraging, so circumscribing, even circumventing, that, although created by antecedent fellow-men, they have on them no stamp of thorough workmanship, but look like the botchery of green apprentices. Thence, those original natures, — and they are the creative centers, the uplifters, the inspirers of humanity, — who by thoughtful prevision and wise practice do what betters and brightens circumstances for those who follow them, become the especially blessed benefactors of their kind. To this sanative class belonged Amalia. With such strong sense of duty, and with so much administrative capacity did this youthful woman conduct the affairs of the duchy, that she warded off any disastrous consequences of the Seven Years' War, bettered the condition of her subjects, and, without additional levy of taxes, accumulated in the treasury a surplus, wherewith she afterwards saved them from the horrors of the famine that afflicted their neighbors.

On a still higher plane even than this did she work. Through perception into the sources of wholesome power, she raised the standard of culture in her capital. The light which makes little Weimar glow to-day, and through all future days, on the map of Germany, with a fire like that of a diamond amid less subtle jewelry, was kindled by the Dowager Duchess Amalia. She gathered around her men of learning and letters. She gave her eldest son, at the age of five years, into the governorship of young Count Goerst, just the right man for the important, delicate duty; and later, she appointed Wieland tutor to her two sons. As Wieland was, in date of establishment in Weimar, the first of that constellation which his pupil Karl August afterwards made to shine as a heaven over the duchy, he demands in this place a few sentences.

Wieland was of a buoyant genial nature, not profound, but comprehensive and impressible. While he owed much of his culture to Addison and Steele, to Gay and Prior, and other English writers of that easy, somewhat shallow age, he, so unequal to Shakespeare in specific weight of understanding, in depth and fullness of poetic sensibility, in penetration and mental power, yet knew so well Shakespeare's worth, that he was the first to make his countrymen acquainted with him through translation ; hereby, as well as by original poems and other writings, proving himself a timely fosterer of German culture and literature. Cicero and Horace he likewise admired, and still more the Greeks, and had in his composition so much of French quality, that he has been called the German Voltaire, a designation which must be taken only to signify a certain superficial versatility and vivacity. With all his want of intellectual solidness and æsthetic depth, Wieland was an earnest man and a moral ; as Goethe said of him, he delighted to play with his conceptions but not with his opinions. Prolific he was in body and mind, having produced fourteen children and fifty volumes. A mild Epicurean in his philosophy, Wieland was in his life as pure and simple as a child.

To a superior feminine nature, just entering womanhood (and to a masculine in hardly less degree), with a good intellect quickened by the

2

mobility and susceptibility of her sex, the world
is at first a kaleidoscope, which at every movement shifts the alluring picture, and ever raises
expectations which are mostly baffled.   Were
young hopes always fulfilled, advancing youth
would be materialized and debased ; for these
hopes are oftenest earthly and worldly.   Their
fulfillment would shut down the horizon of
life, inclose the young mind within itself, thus
slackening and perverting its growth, and
would harden it into unsympathetic egoism.
As humanity is as yet organized, disappointment is its rectifier, its chastener, one might
almost say, its guardian angel.

Of this guardianship Charlotte had her share.
The constraints and adversities, however, that
bore upon her were not of a kind to misguide
her tendencies ; nor were her spontaneous
movements of that passionate sort that lead
sometimes to suicidal rebellion.   In her, " blood
and judgment " were well commingled.   Above
her, in close contact with her, was the Duchess
Amalia.   The social supremacy of a superior
person is a general benefit.   Of this benefit
the most direct rays fell on Charlotte.   When,
through personal gifts, like those of Amalia,
the influence is elevating, an acknowledged

superiority is as serviceable to the minds of those upon whom it acts as the steady force of healthy air is to the body, whose parts it holds firmly together by outward pressure, while feeding it inwardly through the lungs.

II.

MARRIAGE.

FOR those just entering manhood or womanhood the air is as full of love as the earth is
of sunshine on a June morning. At that gor-
geous season the mind regales itself with its
own fragrance, the richest aroma being wafted
from vague, pure, intersexual longings. Joyfully is built a future with the gossamer tissue
of untangled imaginations, which in ninety-
nine cases out of a hundred are sure to be
shivered by the first close contact with reality. In the creative hopefulness of the period
the adolescent are like rejoicing poets, and
ply their fanciful productivity with the eager-
ness which is the charm of poetic work.
Their work, however, is hardly genuine, for it
does not take root ; it is but easy fruitless play,
like games, which end with themselves and
plant nothing. Still the play of young imaginations, by its activity and its very innocence,
feeds inward growth, and may be looked upon
as an aurora that heralds warm future possibili-

ties to the race, when reality shall have become so unfolded and arrayed as no longer to be a pall to glowing expectations.

Charlotte was not one to dizzy herself with excess of imagination : from the first, a clear understanding sobered her thoughts and projects. She was not what is called romantic, a condition where, the wings being too large for the body, the fancy outruns the reason, and cannot help wafting us into impracticable positions. Waking dreams she had, and being a woman, the chief figure in the liveliest of them was a husband. When in her twenty-first year she became a bride, the conversion of nuptial imaginations into fact was by no means a shock ; for, the real husband, Baron von Stein, was the handsome, graceful, showy, sprightly master of the horse, a man of the world, six years her senior, a favorite at court, with business talent, and the possessor of a castle in the neighborhood. Much above this reality would not soar most maidenly ideals, where titles and castles are apt to be prominent features. By the court of Weimar and all " society " the baron was deemed just the real ideal for Charlotte, and Charlotte for him. Pre-ordained was the match, inevitable, in the circle of a small court a necessitated event.

These two not coming together were a disruption of fitness. " Everybody " said it ought to be.

The baron was master of himself. To the parents of Charlotte such a match was, of course, desirable ; to the father, because to a circumscribed old marshal the most conspicuous young noble at this court, who was a man of some character, and inheritor of an ancient *chateau* and domain, was a mate for his daughter almost beyond the field of his expectations, or even hopes. To the dutiful, watchful mother a worthy nobleman, endowed with worldly goods, could not but be acceptable as a suitor for a portionless eldest daughter, who, under an exacting father, had not an enjoyable home. And Charlotte herself probably yielded to all these public, courtly, and domestic influences as much as to any very decided preference for the baron.

And so, on the eighth of May, 1764, the marriage ceremony was performed in the ducal palace, in presence of the whole approving court. And when, in the following March, Charlotte became a mother, among the fifty sponsors at the christening of her first-born son Karl, were the duchess regent, Amalia, the nine year old crown-prince, Karl August, the crown-prince of Gotha, the Duke and Duchess of Coburg, the Prince and Princess of Rudolstadt.

Charlotte was now launched on the career of baroness and mother. From the position of lady-in-waiting to the Duchess Amalia she retired, continuing, however, as wife of one high court functionary and daughter of another, to be closely connected with the court circle. The maternal vocation, — plied so actively that in ten years she gave birth to seven children, — was a joy and a grief to her ; for she had to bear the loss of three daughters, two as infants and one in its fifth year, besides two infant boys. To her earnest, motherly nature this was a great affliction. She suffered also in body to such a degree that, twenty-five years later, referring to this period, she wrote, in a letter to the wife of Schiller : " Wearied with weeping I fell asleep, to drag myself, on waking, through another day ; and heavy lay the thought on me, wherefor Nature had put this affliction upon one half of the race. On account of it, to women should be granted many other privileges of life, but even in that we have been curtailed ; and it is not perceived that for a thousand little affairs of life, which we have to attend to, is needed more faculty (for which we get no credit) than for the doings of a genius who earns honor and fame."

Many months of each year Charlotte spent at her husband's castle of Kochberg, which lay among hills in the neighborhood of Rudolstadt, about fifteen miles from Weimar. The roomy, somewhat gloomy, old castle, whose towers were reflected in the clear water of a pond that glistened around it, had a fine park and gardens, with woody walks and cheerful seats and corners near the gateway. Her resources of music and drawing and reading, the company of her children, a love of seclusion engendered by maternal sorrows, gave to the place a charm which lasted through a long life.

The fast following losses which the affectionate mother had to meet well-nigh robbed Charlotte of all joy in life. To bear her up she had the expansive resources of a strong, earnest, self-sustaining nature. The Duchess Regent Amalia was also strong in intellect, earnest, and self-reliant in character; but she had what her former maid of honor had not to the same degree, hearty enjoyment in the external, in festive recreation. Lacking the finer inwardness of Charlotte, she could not give all the sympathy that Charlotte, in her bereavements,

wanted from a friend. The recreations of the duchess were more superficial, more animal, those of Charlotte more intellectual. Amalia, with all her ableness as regent, her decision and judgment and self-possession, reveled in a release from etiquette and princely restrictions. At times she gave in to convivialities that must have pulled painfully at the very heartstrings of the old marshal, Charlotte's father. Nor must this be thrown up as a reproach; it is rather a proof of the breadth and geniality and genuineness of her being.

In Charlotte's husband there was a still deeper lack of inwardness. Human beings, as to their mental quality, might be broadly divided into two classes, — those whose minds breed upon themselves, and those in whom there is no such interior self-moved productivity, — the prolific and the barren, the minority and the majority. Many worthy, estimable, useful, capable people belong to the majority ; Iago is of the minority. But in most cases the productiveness springs from liveliness of hale sensibilities, which, moving the intellect to imaginative effort, cause an inward vigilance that nourishes the mind and keeps it in repair, and when the organization is large and fine, tends to poetic production. Such minds are mostly sympathetic; among them the genuine poet finds his appreciators. To this refined inwardness Charlotte owed the best of her joys. In solitude it fed her thought with fresh images, it enlarged and renewed her sympathies, it inspirited her to literary study and music. Like Madame du Deffand, and all original clear minds, Charlotte drew herself out of herself. Madame du Deffand, says Sainte-Beuve, was of all persons the one who the least asked her neighbors how she should think.

This interior sanctuary the baron had not the delicate key to open. His life was in the external and the superficial; he could not put himself into subtle relation with the self-cultivating woman whose sensibilities were her wealth. His duties, moreover, kept him much from home and away from Weimar. He dined at court every day. A handsome, graceful exterior, with superficial amiabilities of bearing, is sometimes a captivating mask that hides interior deformities. This was not the case with Stein; he was only hollow, not vicious or illtempered. The baron was neither coarse nor corrupt, but he had no inward vision.

The Duchess Amalia, having abandoned the purpose of sending to a high school her two boys, the crown-prince and his brother, ap-

pointed, in 1772, Wieland to be their instructor.
Through the authoritative influence of Amalia,
Weimar had already entered the path of self-
improvement ; by this appointment that path
was suddenly smoothed and brightened. By
the active presence of a cultivated genius the
aspiring are emboldened. To all who have the
eyes to see it, the flame which ascends from
the kindling of disinterested thought in the
poet and scholar is a pillar of light. Amid the
impulsions of greedy passion, the earnest, un-
excited, yet highly practical life of such a man
is a purifying predominance. Wieland, though
not one of the enduring masters, like Kant and
Goethe, — minds in which humanity through
all time can seek for solutions and steep itself for renewal, — was, nevertheless, a man of
genius, and a genuine literary worker, one who
wrought from inward motion ; and he was
blessed with that gentle enthusiasm, that latent warmth, which quickens the poetic temperament, and whose activity is needed for the
production of that, than which, says Joubert,
nothing is more beautiful, a beautiful book.
He was then the most admired poet of Germany ; for this was two or three years before
" Goetz von Berlichingen " and " Werther " had
with a burst of thunder music announced the
supreme genius of the age.

A general good to the community, the advent of such a man was an especial boon to Charlotte. Although Wieland's Epicurean sensibilities lacked the grasping strength to couple themselves to the deeper, more Christian sensibilities of Charlotte, and she in her intercourse with him could not look for full reciprocation, the complacent vivacity of his nature, his communicativeness and knowledge and culture, made him to her at once an attractive and instructive companion. Wieland was, if not profound, so freshly productive that he deserved the high title awarded him by Goethe as one of the educators of his age. Genial and sociable, there was, together with his cultivation, a wholeness about him seldom met with even in superior men, who are sometimes the more one-sided for their very proficiencies. Halfness is not only a common characteristic of educated people, but it is at times attended by what is much worse than itself, — a pretension to wholeness.

So broken was Charlotte in health that in the summer of 1773 she betook her to the baths of Pyrmont, then, with the exception of Spa, the most frequented watering-place in Germany. Thither resorted annually, from neighboring Hanover, where he was court physician,

Dr. Zimmermann. The doctor came for a few weeks of midsummer to gather the harvest that ripened for a popular practitioner on the ailments of the titled and the wealthy. The service thus done the doctor by Pyrmont he was enabled to repay; for, if the reputed curative virtue of the water was the original source of attraction to visitors, the doctor's reputation grew to be an important adjunct, many invalids traveling to Pyrmont because there they could profit by the skill of Dr. Zimmermann. His skill consisted in doing as little harm as possible to his patients, and in discerning that change of air, restriction in diet, respite from home anxieties, with the self-repairing resources of nature, are the efficient agents of improvement in frequenters of fashionable wateringplaces. Zimmermann was a cultivated man of the world, who could make himself acceptable in the best company. His medical was reinforced by his literary reputation. Besides professional books, he was the author of a then noted one on National Pride, and a still more noted one on Solitude. "Zimmermann on Solitude" is a volume which some of my older readers may have had in their hands more than fifty years ago, as it had the honor of translation into English, an honor due probably to

friendly relations bred between the author and
influential British subjects of George III., at
the English court of Hanover. With all his
temporary vogue as doctor and author, Zimmermann was evidently a man of insight and
just perception. He soon came to know the
worth of Charlotte, an appreciation in which
he was aided by the judgment of the high company at Pyrmont, who quickly apprehended her
distinction.

The year 1774 was a year of trials. The
ducal palace caught fire and was burnt to
ashes, and along with it the theater. To a
small, concentrated community like Weimar,
this was an aggravated infliction. The court
could in a few days nestle itself in a new home ;
not so the stage, dependent too on the court
for sustenance. The theater was a general
loss ; an especial one to Charlotte, who often
sought it, as well for recreation as distraction.
In this year the mother's heart was again des-
olated by the death of an infant daughter.
About the same time took place the marriage
of her sister Louise to Major von Imhoff, a
marriage which, approved by the bride's family, could not but cause some misgivings to
Louise's experienced sister.

Imhoff was one of those cometary individuals

who, by their erratic orbit and strange cor-
ruscations, startle the onlooking world, and
threaten to shake old Custom from his proprie-
ties. Like their sidereal prototypes, they seem
eccentric, because we do not yet know the law
of their motion and being. Was Imhoff an
adventurer? Your adventurer is one who not
only uses the world as a capital out of which
to draw dividends of success, but whose agents
for manipulating this capital are audacity and
impudence, — a pair that, either by their co-
operation generate unscrupulousness, or by it
are wrought into efficient copartnership. The
adventurer makes of circumstances expedient
opportunities, using them purely for the better-
ing of his worldly condition.

Christian Adam Karl von Imhoff began his
career as groom of the bedchamber at the
court of Würtemberg, rose to the rank of
major in the Seven Years' War, and being, at
the end of the war, honorably discharged,
turned to account his pictorial talent, and as
portrait-painter came to Nuremberg, where the
charms of Marianne Chapuset, just budding
into womanhood, so captivated him that he,
then about thirty years of age, married the
daughter of a corporal's poor widow, herein
showing more of passionate precipitancy than

of the calculating self-command which con-
duces so much to the prosperity of the accomplished adventurer.   In the hope of cultivating
a more fertile professional field, he soon moved
from Nuremberg to London, and in 1769,
with a similar aim, he took ship for Madras.
Among the passengers was Warren Hastings,
member of the India Council.

Besides more than common beauty of form
and feature, heightened by feminine grace,
Marianne had a sprightly mind, with German
naturalness and feminine softness.   On ship-
board, where all are ever very near neighbors,
and especially on an India voyage in this unavoidable close proximity for weeks and months,
a young woman thus richly endowed was a
danger to a widower of thirty-seven, and he a
man of strong, impassioned, concentrated nature, as was Warren Hastings.   And when this
hourly neighborhood of place began, the neighborhood of feeling between Marianne and Imhoff had ceased.   On her part it had never ex-
isted.   With little of the attachment which is
implied in a genuine marriage, she had accepted
Imhoff, just as many an undowered girl gives
her hand without her whole heart to a man
above her in station or in fortune.   In the yet
but partially developed state of human associa-

tion, multiform are the compulsions and un-
healthy obediences to which men, and still
more women, have to submit themselves. On
his part, Imhoff had hastily married a stranger
from passion, which had not ripened into domestic affection, and he soon discovered that a
penniless wife was to him a burden and a hindrance. The mutual devotion that grew between Marianne and Hastings caused him no
heartache ; and when, towards the end of the
voyage, a divorce was proposed, and Hastings,
to secure his concurrence, offered a large sum
of gold, Imhoff readily gave in to the proposal.
In Germany, at that period, divorces were frequent, and easily obtained. Public sentiment
justified them ; the law authorized them. They
were often granted where incompatibility and
alienation in the old union, and affection and
congeniality in the new, were far less conspicuous than in the present instance.

To Imhoff, indeed, Hastings was a godsend,
and for him his wife became suddenly a brilliant match. She was to give him his liberty
(and that no other person in the world could
do), and at the same time (O doubly dowered
woman !) the means to make liberty delectable.
Until the divorce should be obtained Imhoff
and Marianne were to continue together. The

needed documents reached India from Germany just as Hastings was appointed governor-general and had moved from Madras to Calcutta. He adopted the two children of Marianne and Imhoff, who were thus not separated from their mother, and he had the marriage rites solemnized that made him and Marianne man and wife according to the requirements of the English church and state. The captivating, accomplished daughter of a Würtemberg corporal entered upon a career of almost regal grandeur and power for which she was not unfitted. Imhoff, the liberated, the enriched, the rejoicing, returned to Germany, there to be helped in getting another wife, and she of noble lineage, by the wealth he had got for parting with his first plebeian wife; and to be helped too by Rumor, who, ever apt at multiplication, had cried him about as one of the richest of nabobs.

III.

BETWEEN Zimmermann and his fair Weimar patient, after her departure from Pyrmont, there was interchange of letters; and "Werther" having just appeared, Charlotte wrote of her admiration of it, with misgivings as to the nature of its influence, and expressed a wish, — universally felt just then, especially by the women of Germany, — to become acquainted with the author. Zimmermann, in return, says that he had been so profoundly wrought upon by "Werther" that, after finishing the first part, he had to pause a fortnight before going on with the second, and prophetically adds: "You wish to see him; but, dear friend, you have no thought of how dangerous this captivating lovable man may become to you."

In the summer of 1775 Goethe, coming out of Switzerland, fell in with Zimmermann on the upper Rhine. Zimmermann, in aid of his eulogies, showed Goethe a silhouette of Charlotte. The portrait, — its own light further in-

flamed by praises of the original, — made such
an impression on Goethe that Zimmermann, —
evidently liable to the seduction of hyperbole,
— writes to Charlotte, that Goethe had been
kept awake by it for three nights. Under the
silhouette Goethe wrote : " It were a glorious
sight to see how the world mirrors itself in this
soul. She sees the world as it is, and yet
through the medium of love. The pervading
impression is softness."

On passing through Frankfort Zimmermann
was the guest of Goethe, and writes of him to
Charlotte: " In Frankfort I stayed with Mr.
Goethe, one of the most extraordinary and
powerful geniuses that ever appeared on the
earth," — words which to every one would then
have seemed swollen with extravagance, but
which are now known to be words of unexag-
gerated truth, whose utterance at that moment
bears witness to the discernment of the writer.

By the portrait Goethe was moved to send
to Lavater a professional letter. Goethe, whose
grasping, hungry mind nothing escaped, had,
through personal intimacy with Lavater, taken
hold of the fanciful inferences and ingenious
conjectures which Lavater was vainly striving
to shape into a science of physiognomy. With
his keen perception and plastic creativeness,

Goethe could doubtless make more of an expressive countenance than could his superficial friend, the inventor. Here is the letter, written in the summer of 1775 : —

" How did Zimmermann get on ? Where is he ? When he comes back he must lodge with me : forget not to write him this. Beg H. Schulz to let thee have a few silhouettes of my phiz, and send them to me by the first opportunity. Hast thou been at work on the book, and wilt send me something soon ? Here are comments on the silhouettes of Baroness von Stein and Marchioness Branconi.

STEIN.

Steadfastness : complacent persistent dwelling on a subject : satisfaction with herself : attractive amiability : naiveté and goodness, fluent speech : gentle constancy : fidelity : conquers with nets.

BRANCONI.

Enterprising strength : keen but not deep : pure vanity : subtle exacting affability : wit, cultivated speech : choice in expression : resistance : self-esteem : grasping and tenacious : conquers with arrows.

" I should like thee to leave these to me, with Frau von Loew, for the second part : they

should be well engraved. I will make comments on them, send them to thee for remarks,
and then finish them. The whole of the second
part should be done in this way. But thou
uncertain one!"

The vitality there is in these physiognomical
ventures is not greater than their faithfulness
of portraiture. They are more than good hits
guided by common report and the indications
of Zimmermann. They are stamped with that
vividness and fidelity which can only be reached
by the spiritual grasp of sympathy enlivened
by poetic feeling. Creative genius leaps to the
peaks of human being, and from these heights
peers into the depth of character, into the very
abysses that darken round the base.

On the seventh of November, 1775, Goethe
arrived in Weimar. Before following him
thither let us give some lines to a question
that is sometimes raised : Was Goethe's going to Weimar a gain to himself and to Germany ?

Frankfort or Weimar : the thought to be set
as basis to such a discussion is, that Goethe
was a born genius, by nature fitted out with
rare gifts and exceptional mental power, who
therefore would have grown to distinction anywhere. Could his great faculties be best un-

folded in a free city where, so far from there
being a reigning duke and titled adherents,
there was not in the circuit of the town an individual man with inherited honors, no *Herr
von*, no baron, no count, and especially no
prince ruling by transmitted right; but instead,
only temporary life-titles, self-given by burgh-
ers for public services within their precincts,
the citizens governed by a senate of their own
choosing ; would a Goethe have broader, freer
scope for the fructification and maturing of his
genius in republican Frankfort or in monarchic,
aristocratic Weimar ?

Here it must be borne in mind that the free
city of Frankfort had no real self-subsistence.
Politically it was dependent on the German
empire, whose Diet dwelt within its gates,
whose emperors were crowned in its cathe-
dral. What kind of a republic could a town
of sixty thousand inhabitants be that was the
capital of an immense empire made up of imperial royalists, kingdoms, large and small,
principalities, duchies? It had the body of a
republic but not the soul. It nurtured no
strong, lively political life, — that self-sustained
life which, imparting vigor of character and
courage, enlivens an independent selfhood, and
prompts to bold initiatives. No Athenian at-

mosphere blew bracing there to swell some
patriot's breast to the robustness of a Miltiades
or a Demosthenes.   On the market-place no
Socrates was encountered, no Plato, no Alcibi-
ades.   Frankfort had the honor of giving birth
to Goethe: it could not give him companions.
In all high directions it was circumscribed, un-'
developed.   To stimulate mind, to quicken aspiration, there was nothing.

Moreover, through its fairs Frankfort had
grown to be a trading center, and as a consequence of this, as well as from its topographical
position and imperial eminence, was a chief
seat of banking.   The Rothchilds originated
here.   Necessary as bankers may be in the
mechanism of modern commerce, the atmosphere in which they thrive is not the one to
expand the lungs of literature.   Where they
most do congregate is generated a virtual materialism, and this is the most deadly foe to the
mounting thought of pure letters.   In a large
capital the banking element is fractional, subordinate; in a small town it is predominant.   The
rich bankers of Frankfort were the most important personages in it.   In a wealth-worship-
ing society young ambitions are launched
upon the current that flows towards wealth's
success.   What is ever most prominently be-

fore the eyes of a community gets to be its
chief educator: men learn through their daily
desires. In its rank effluvia mammonism
smothers the upflaming spirit of disinterested
literary thought.

At sixteen Goethe was sent from Frankfort
to the University of Leipzig. Here his principal studies were of human nature in his fellow-
creatures and himself, — studies pursued with
most zest, and for him, the embryo poet, with
most return, in the streets and theaters and
wine-cellars and beer-gardens and boarding-
houses of lively Leipzig. Here he again fell
in love (he was all his life liable to the falls
caused by this delightful intoxication), and love
was to him an instructive expositor. From the
lecture-rooms the only pleasant and durable
memory he brought away was of Oeser, to
whom, for having put him thus early on the
right æsthetic track, he was ever grateful.
From Leipzig his father sent him (to complete
his academic law-knowledge) to the University
of Strasburg. Here, besides earning a degree
as Doctor of Laws, he continued his love-ex-
periences, — in a way that has brought upon
him the unremitted reprehension, together with
the forgiveness, of the gentler, the forgiving
sex, — and had entrance opened to him into the

boundless world of Shakespeare. This, working upon adventurous native genius, quickly
led to the production of "Goetz von Berlichingen," written when Goethe was twenty-two.
In the spring of 1772, — his father being pater-
nally bent on making a great jurist of him, — he
arrived in Wetzlar, then the seat of the highest
judicial tribunal of Germany. Here he resumed his love-studies, with such earnestness
that he burnt into his heart the materials for
" Werther " — that firebrand hurled defiantly by
agonized genius, to set all Germany in flames.

It was by going away from his native town
(and it would have been the same had his
native town been Manheim or Cologne instead
of Frankfort) that Goethe got the enlargement
and the stimulus to produce "Goetz" and "Werther." One effect of these was acquaintance
with the young Duke of Weimar. Suppose that
his sudden fame had brought Goethe an invitation to visit the Elector of Hesse at Cassel, or
the court of Hanover, or that of Gotha or
of Dresden. Probably he would have accepted
the invitation ; but there is little probability
that a visit would have been turned into a resi
dence. In not one of these courts was there
the environment that could have narrowed and
strengthened itself into a clasp of sympathy and

love to hold close to its breast such a man and such a genius. Not one of them could have been more to him than a kindly condescending patron. Goethe patronized! A patron Goethe would not have borne for a day. Would you be assured of this, read " Goetz " and " Werther." As soon would a cherub submit to the petting of gnomes. But he was not invited by any one of them, and he was by the Duke of Weimar. How did this come about?

We have seen what kind of woman was the mother of the duke, the Dowager Duchess Amalia, a unique princess, self-dedicated to the higher duties, capable of the higher things. Of her son, Karl August, when a boy of fourteen, Frederick the Great said, he " had never seen a young man of his age who inspired such hopes." Karl August began his manhood as his father had done and with a like success: he went a-wooing, and brought home from Darmstadt a bride, as his father had brought one from Brunswick. On the journey, moved by the example of his mother and an inward sympathy with genius, the young duke sought Goethe. On meeting, the two were drawn one to the other. The personal fascination of Goethe, especially in his earlier manhood, has often been mentioned by contem-

poraries ; the duke, too, was magnetic. Goethe's
father, looking upon Weimar as one of the
common petty courts of Germany, was averse
to his son's accepting the invitation of the
duke ; and had Weimar been a common German court, he would assuredly have been
right.

Karl August, become of age as ducal sovereign at eighteen, brought shortly after to
Weimar his consort, Louise, worthy to be the
peer of his mother Amalia, and his tutor Wieland, and his governor, Count Goertz. What
German court or city of that day could show
such a quintette for the performance of the divine music of high work and high thought ?
And this choice band was to be strengthened
by a sixth, flushed with the glory of "Goetz" and
"Werther," aglow with the soul's warmth out
of which they had sprung. Goethe, the youthful, the beautiful, the captivating genius, would
have found admirers, friends, anywhere in Germany: in Weimar he had admirers, friends, and
sympathetic appreciators. Here was opened to
him a free field and fullest scope. He found,
what the poet so seldom finds, intelligent sympathy. A center of radiating light, he was
surrounded by admirers who were capable of
being enlightened. His rich personality and

genial powers had clean play. This was a joy and a rare good fortune. From the first Goethe was a willing teacher as well as learner, and here he found people ready to be taught. He became at once the acknowledged chief aristocrat in a circle of aristocrats. What is an aristocrat?

The word, like many other good words, we owe to those practical idealists, the great Greeks. That to be governed by the best men would be the best government they readily perceived, and so, after their high fashion, they coined the noble word which signifies that rule. The word is all the nobility there is. The thing signified has so degenerated that the dictionaries define *aristocracy* to be "a form of government which places the supreme power in the hands of the principal persons of a state," thus putting the sham in the place of the true, the usurper on the seat of the legitimate owner. Nor has the degradation stopped there; for the second definition given by Worcester of *aristocrat* is "a haughty or overbearing person." Nay, the debasement has gone lower still, and in certain places, in the minds of certain people, by aristocracy is meant the richest citizens.

In their struggle upwards the Greeks vainly

strove to make the noble word a permanent
thing. The futility of the effort was glaringly
exhibited when the Athenian "aristocrats" put
to death Socrates, the best and greatest man
that Athens, so affluent in great men, had ever
produced. There is no record of a state where
there has been, except momentarily, a government conducted by the best men. Not in Rome
any more than in Athens, neither in Venice
nor in Florence, was there ever other than an
approximation of the thing to the word. The
reign of the Antonines seems to shake this
position. Theirs was rule by a single head.
The monarchical aristocracy of a Marcus Aure-
lius is incomparably preferable to the monarchical brutality of a Commodus; but there can be
no best government (only comparatively good)
without the agency of all the wisest in its administration; and for that the whole national
mass must be quickened by a feeling of ruler's
responsibility, a responsibility so wakeful, intelligent, and true that through it are lifted to
the top the fittest for conducting public affairs.
The British house of peers, — so important for
the part it has played in England, whose national development presents the most thorough
and instructive exemplification of political evolution presented by history, — the house of

peers is not a genuine aristocracy. Its five
hundred members are not the five hundred
best and wisest men of the British empire.
Nature rejects, — I had almost said, indignantly rejects, — aristocracy by family trans-
mission. Nor, in the present phase of human
development, is perfect harmony between the
word and the thing by any means attained
through election. A scrutiny of our own public assemblies, and especially of the municipal
governments of our cities, will prove that. The
most genuinely aristocratic legislative body
that ever met was the American Congress of
1776, " those fifty-six who signed as one." Under the strong inward heave of great principles,
under the still deeper ground-swell that was unconsciously maturing a momentous new epoch
in human history, the best men were lifted
into that august assemblage. Washington and
Franklin, Samuel Adams and Jefferson, Pat-
rick Henry and John Adams, Livingston and
Rutledge, Randolph and Sherman, Middleton
and Rush, Chase and Ellery, and their bold
fellow-members, were distinguished aristocrats.

This aristocratic superiority is independent
of birth. Nature bestows it impartially on
peasant and king. Luther and John Knox
were higher aristocrats than even Gustavus

Adolphus and William the Silent. Out of the social anomalies and political solecisms which still almost make confusion instead of order predominant, we are gradually working our way into conditions of healthier life, where the fittest will by all men be recognized and placed in due position to do the highest public work, as surely as in games the foremost now always are by boys on the play-ground. In the mean time, we have often to bear with second-class men in first places, and at times with eminent one-sided workers who assume to be many-sided. Napoleon was monstrously one-sided, only an aristocrat militarily, by deep dark moral deficiencies incompetent as a statesman and civil ruler. Louis Napoleon was not an aristocrat on any side.

In Weimar, towards the end of 1775, the word and the thing *aristocracy* were more har-monized than anywhere else in Germany. The young duke, Karl August, had just taken into his hands the reins of sovereignty, — he who had had the sagacious high-toned Count Goertz for governor, the poet Wieland for tu-tor, and the practical, dutiful Amalia for mother, and who was by nature intellectually well en-dowed, and morally honest, energetic, impas-sioned. His youthful consort, Louise, was fully equal to her distinguished destiny. She had enough clear, high qualities to value Goethe ; and he, through fifty years, was her faithful friend, at times of trial befriending her with his high conduct and fraternal sympathy.

At that time the numerous German States were despotisms, tempered by advancing culture ; each state controlled by one will ; and if this happened to lodge in a selfish brute, his subjects were sold to a foreign king, to be slain on distant battle-fields, fighting unconsciously against freedom. Or, if that will lodged in the brain of a Karl August, he sought to do the best that could be done for his subjects, calling to his side qualified men, and placing at their head the greatest man Germany possessed, whom he, the duke, had the sympathetic insight thus early to appreciate.

In Weimar, with Karl August, Goethe had what he could not have had anywhere else, — full play for all his gifts. Fullness of expansion perfects individual aptitudes. The poet must have a visionary eye, the faculty of beholding real things imaginatively, but the better his opportunities of intimately seeing men in earnest action, the truer, clearer, more mellow and various will be his poetic representations of humanity. Had Shakespeare

4

never gone beyond the limits of Warwickshire, he would still have been a marvelous poet, but one-sided, incomplete : he never would have produced "Hamlet" or "Macbeth." He got his rich culture (rich, because of his interior wealth) in swarming, strenuous London, the London of Elizabeth and Raleigh, of Bacon and Sidney.   \

Goethe's was a mind of the highest method. His hours and his work were ordered and apportioned, else he never could have marshaled his numerous, restless, interior forces. This gave him time for all things without strain or fatigue. "Faust" and "Wilhelm Meister" were deepened and broadened and rounded by their author's nine or ten early years of statesmanship. His close practical contact with many and divers men stimulated and tempered his faculties, trained his literary vision ; his continuous discipline of the capable, impetuous duke was a productive self-discipline. At the same time he was educating his official co-workers and all the men and women about him who were susceptible of high influences ; and doing all this by the free action of his strong, ardent, earnest mind. No man is freer than such a willing, various worker, moving under command of duty and love, guided by calm genius, as no man is less free than the willing idler. These were the conditions (conditions wrought out by his own power and will, making the most of favoring circumstances) in which to unfold his manifold manhood. *Voilà un homme,* said Napoleon, after an interview with Goethe ; and his exclamation has a meaning deeper than he meant or could give. This true, full, genuine man encouraged and led the circle about him in Weimar, having the necessary prerequisite and privilege of an intellectual atmosphere, which was warmed by love and admiration for him, — an atmosphere in which he created the works in whose enduring pages the aspiring spirits of Christendom find ever encouragement and illumination.

IV.

THE visionary portraits, one of the other, which for several months Charlotte and Goethe had caressed, were not dissolved by their meeting. The fancy-fed pictures proved rather to be inanimate likenesses, which, when the originals confronted each other, glistened suddenly with captivating life, as a sleeping beauty would on awaking into the gaze of an admiring beholder, quickening his admiration into delighted wonder at her blazing eyes and ravishing motions. Their coming into mutual presence was a fulfillment, not a disappointment. In each a soulful individuality was brightened by intellectual intentness. While both drew people to them wherever they appeared, each had sides of especial fascination to the other. Goethe's allurements had been hitherto those of an ardent young man to very young girls. A mature, fully-formed woman he had not yet come in contact with as lover. Charlotte von Stein was to him a new, and on that very account, an inviting experience, — an earnest, disciplined woman of the world, brought up in a cultivated court, through position and surroundings a woman of rank, through intrinsic refinement a graceful, high-bred lady. That in her expressive, very pleasing, not beautiful, countenance there was a tinge of the mystery of sorrow, gave it a subtle finishing enticement to a sympathetic nature like Goethe's, especially at that moment, when out of his own heart's trials he had been creating "Werther," and when that heart still vibrated with the pain of parting from Lili in Frankfort.

Goethe's strong attraction towards women made him very attractive to them ; and here was a woman whose heart had been balked of its hopes, in whom the feelings of an aspiring womanly nature had nourished themselves upon inbred ideals. Like other educated women of that day, she had read, and with more penetration than most readers, what Goethe had already published. And now, long heralded by friends as one especially fitted for her sympathy and admiration, appears in person the author of "Werther," his great, shining, wonderful eyes beaming upon her with the interest and admiration — one might almost say, intimacy — they had brought from her portrait and

the confidences of Zimmermann. The brilliancy,
freshness, heartiness of his talk, — never more
sparkling and cordial than when addressed
to engaging women, — falling on an ear pre-
possessed for it, with the captivation of his
bearing and manly beauty, could not but
powerfully impress a woman susceptible, as
Charlotte was, of the higher admirations. She
was in her thirty-third year, seven years older
than Goethe, and through him there was kindled in her the light of thoughts and feelings
which renewed her youth, and requited her for
long-baffled expectations.

Goethe arrived in Weimar on the seventh of
November, 1775. This will be the place for
a note he sent to Merck, in Darmstadt, just
before leaving Frankfort.

"I expect the duke and Louise, and go
with them to Weimar. There we shall have
again all kinds of good and whole and half
things, which may God make helpful to us.
Meanwhile, farewell, old fellow, and make the
best of life. Canst thou send me ten carolins [a carolin is about five dollars] : I have
need of them. I have translated the Song of
Solomon, which is the most glorious collection
of love-songs that God ever created. La Roche
is doing penance because thou dost not answer

her. Ride over here once more before I go. I am tolerably. Have written much at " Faust." Zimmermann greets thee ; he passed through Darmstadt in the night. Greet wife and children."

The request for ten carolins is a dun. Merck, one of Goethe's early friends, whom, on account of his mocking speech and negative turn of mind, he used to call Mephistopheles Merck, was a bright fellow and a distinguished critic in literature and art, but an insatiate borrower.

Goethe came to Weimar for a visit of a few weeks ; he came to give himself a holiday, to have a frolic. The frolic was wilder than he had looked for. The duke, — who, but for the sovereign's privilege of premature legal manhood at eighteen, would have been still a boy, — just freed from the bonds of governors and guardians, with excess of that impulsive force which is an element in the mature greatness of men of action, was delightfully intoxicated by the companionship of Goethe, who, arriving from Frankfort a still heartaching lover, was just in the mood to drown the past in an effervescence of present fun and extravagance.

The quiet community stared at the mad pranks of the witty revelers. These danced

and caroused and masqueraded and played
plays and awoke astonished echoes in the
neighboring hills with the huntsman's horn in
midwinter. By their boisterous irregularities
the court was somewhat disorganized. The
elders shook their heads ; the earnest, high-
toned Count Goertz was almost angered. The
young bride, Duchess Louise, with her native
sense of propriety and princely dignity, was
so much discomposed that, notwithstanding her
prepossession in favor of Goethe, she would
have harbored unfriendly thoughts towards him
as the misleader of her youthful husband, and
as one of whom, too, for drawing him away
from her, she had cause to be jealous, but for
Charlotte, between whom and Louise, through
elevated partialities and refined affinities, was
formed an early, life-long friendship. With
Charlotte Goethe soon became unreservedly
confidential. As the intimacy between them
strengthened, she failed not to perceive, through
the glow of youthful exuberance and the gush
of animal spirits, the earnestness and uprightness of his nature, and that central solidity
which was the core of his future greatness. In
answer to a letter from her, giving an account
of Goethe's reception in Weimar, Zimmermann
wrote her on the twenty-ninth of December,

1775, in his wonted tone of enthusiasm about Goethe, a letter, the latter part of which I give for the sake of the remarkable prophecy with which it concludes : " Wieland's friendship for Goethe is very lovely. Say to Wieland with what joy I behold this new laurel-twig in the wreath that encircles his brow. For Goethe I wish all honor and trust at your court. A courtier (pardon the unnoble expression) of this kind, under a wise, intelligent, enlightened prince, like the duke, can call forth with you a golden age, which shall make an epoch in history, and with posterity extinguish the so-called great deeds of the larger courts and the larger nations."

A few months later, Wieland, in a letter to Merck, speaks of his devotion to Goethe with a warmth which is significant in regard to both, and which gives proof of a nobleness of nature unexampled in this kind in literature. Can there be found another instance of a popular poet who, at the height of fame and vigor of age (Wieland was then forty-three), shows such love for a young rising rival, and such enjoyment of his brilliant success ? This is the passage : " Our Goethe has again, through his " Stella," gloriously manifested himself to the world. How my heart triumphs at every

new victory that he gains, every new province
that he conquers. Do you know of another
example where one poet has loved another so
enthusiastically? I almost believe that it may
come from this, that I, in comparison with him,
am only a weak clod of earth. For does not
Plato say, the beloved is rich and the lover
poor? And is not Plato right? Let it pass:
my heart is thus, and enough, that it makes me
happy." And a fortnight later, March 25th,
1776, Wieland writes to Merck that Goethe has
hired a house, and will never quit Weimar during the duke's life, even should that stretch to
the length of Nestor's; and he ends the paragraph with these words: "For me life would
now be worth nothing without this wonderful
youth, whom I love as my only-begotten son,
and, as happens with a real father, I have an
inward joy to see how he outgrows me in
height, and is all that which I have not been
able to become."

Censorious comments on Goethe and Karl
August were not confined to Weimar. People
are ever on the watch to catch their fellows
tripping; it is such comfort to find, or to fancy,
one's self better than one's neighbors, and the ·
more favored by fortune the delinquent is, the
sweeter is the pharisaical consolation we ex-

tract out of his aberrations. Gossip could hardly have found swifter carriers than a sovereign duke and the author of "Werther." What they and their free companions were misdoing enlivened the tea-tables of all Germany, and reached the ears of Klopstock in the far north. A pious and moral man, who had achieved poetic fame by celebrating so high a theme as the Messiah, and had written patriotic odes, Klopstock felt that he had an indisputable title, not only to sit in judgment on a young German poet and a very young German duke, but to utter sentence against them. He wrote to Goethe a friendly paternal letter of remonstrance, which Goethe answered kindly but briefly, the purport being that he, Klopstock, had better mind his own business. To this Klopstock retorted a few lines of indignation, telling Goethe he was not worthy of such friendship.

Klopstock might be called a chronological poet ; that is, a poet who owed his temporary eminence to the conditions of the period at which he appeared. His mind had not enough of the swing given to poetic organizations by electric movement, not enough of the fire which, swelling the seized subject into roundness, animates it with a light that resists ex-

tinguishment and refuses to be superseded.
His honest nature was somewhat shadowed by
self-estimation; it had not that finer trans-
lucency that would have enabled him to see
himself in comparison with others. When
Klopstock died, in the beginning of the present
century, at the age of seventy-nine, he seems
to have been totally unaware that he was de-
throned, that

" All the air
Is emptied of thy hoary majesty." [1]

Goethe and Karl August went on their er-
rant way, inly moved by springs somewhat
deeper and more finely tempered than those
which set in motion the tongues and pens of
their censors. The loftier men's natures are,
the more liable are they to invisible aid, to the
power and quality of which they are mostly the
blindest who are the readiest to sit in judgment on their superior fellows. On the deflec-
tions of men of clean, upright aims angels
only smile. The young duke's attachment to
Goethe and admiration of him growing daily
with closer acquaintanceship, he soon consulted
him informally about public affairs, and finding
him as able as he was willing to give counsel,
resorted to him more and more, until by de-

----

[1] Keats.

grees the hours of work encroached upon the hours of play, and soon, play took its proper place as recreation after work, and at last, change of work was found the wholesome mode of recreation. Karl August had the unique privilege of sowing his wild oats with Goethe walking by his side. The boon companion who surpassed the whole crew in the extravagance of his pranks, transformed himself into the wise, methodical, laborious councilor and minister. Montaigne, speaking of the men of his day, says that " he knows a number of men who have diverse gifts to a high degree: one, intellect ; another, heart ; a third, address ; such a one, conscience ; another, science ; more than one, language ; in short, each one has his gift ; but a great man generally, one possessing many fine gifts together, it has not been my fortune to know." Such, indeed, are rare, very rare, — lights sparsely sprinkled along the crepuscular confines of earthly space, upflaming beacons out of unconfined infinity. One of these was Goethe, a man solitary, of infinite instincts, rich to overflowing with the finer juices of humanity.

V.

THE prayer of Socrates, "Grant that we may be inwardly beautiful," like all cordial prayer, gave note of such moral aspiration, that it was a prophecy of its own fulfillment. The pure in heart are prone to fortify resolution with such appeals, not so much that they fear the blight of temptation, as that they know the happiness of purity. If, in her intercourse with Goethe, Charlotte sought to strengthen herself with a similar prayer, it was from a vivid consciousness of her dignity and duty as wife and mother, rather than from any besetting weakness of the woman. Goethe, in his first conversations with her, soon felt that here was a woman whom he could respect and trust as well as love ; and in her, along with esteem and admiration for him, were aroused her best faculties and sympathies ; and these, had her wifely self-reliance needed invigoration, were additional guards to her honor. Charlotte had that thorough self-respect which is the guardian-angel of conduct.

The relation between Goethe and Charlotte during fifty years is depicted in Goethe's letters to her, beginning in 1776, and ending in 1826, filling three volumes, those written in the first ten years of their acquaintance taking up more than two and a half of the three. Her letters to Goethe she withdrew and destroyed.

Those of the first months exhibit the ardent young poet undergoing purgation, obliged to submit to restraint and absence. The familiar *Du* alternates with the formal *Sie*, according as he feels himself repressed or favored. From this let it not be inferred that Charlotte was playing the coquette or he the seducer. She was the opposite of frivolous, and had too much personal dignity and sense of truth to descend to the artifices of coquetry ; and he, by the honesty and healthy warmth of his nature, was incapable of the baseness that seeks to gain by circumvention and art what is not yielded through reciprocation and sympathy.

How could such a woman but become deeply interested in this fiery young poet, full of all that makes opening manhood admirable and lovable. That this distinguished man, the object of universal homage, over whom younger

beauties were striving to throw the net of their
fascinations, had singled her out for warm unremitted devotion, could not but add to his
charm and power. She had no thought of re-
pelling him, but she wished to school his love
into a higher phase. She was performing the
controlling selective part which, in all such re-'
lations, belongs to woman, by virtue of her holy
function of motherhood.

Goethe lived within a stone's throw of the
adored lady ; they met at court and elsewhere,
so that in his notes there are frequent allu-
sions, mostly playful, to small incidents and to
persons. Not only is their tone healthy, but
as mark of this are touches of fun : not a
shade of Wertherian gloom anywhere. Full of
life and genuine feeling are the notes, and at
the same time they are cheerful. In one, on
the twenty-ninth of January, he almost threatens to leave Weimar. Charlotte had written or
told him, that what he thought pure passion
was imaginative self-delusion. He answers :
" Perhaps, too, I deceive myself in believing
that I see when it is day, that I warm myself
at heat, and freeze in frost. All this may be
fancy. Enough for the present that it is so :
when it gets to be otherwise I shall find it out.
The printed *Stella* is come : thou shalt have

a copy. Shouldst love me a little in return. My head and heart are sorely tossed, whether I shall stay or go." Only two days before, in describing to her a fancy ball, he seems to aim at piquing her into jealousy : " Yesterday evening I was at first in a very bad mood. It depressed both the duchess and me that you were not there. The Keller and the pretty Bechtolsheim could not set me a-going. Karl [Charlotte's son] brought me your note ; that made the matter worse : the soles of my feet burned to run to you. At last I began to do what was right, and then I was better. Flirtation is the most approved palliative in such cases. I fibbed all around, and flattered every pretty face, and had the advantage of believing for the moment what I said. The milkmaid pleased me much ; with a little more youth and health she might become dangerous to me."

Between these two notes is a brief one of the twenty-eighth of January, which is worth quoting, it gives so clearly the relation between them, — ardor on his part, reserve and self-reliance on hers. A happy combination is it, when a woman, who possesses the zone of Venus, wears with it what Mr. H. J. Ruggles, in his " Essay on the Method of Shakespeare," calls the " girdle of self-restraint." Here is the

5

note. The letters sent for were to and from his sister, which he had given Charlotte to read: " Dear angel, I am not going to the. concert. For I am so well that I don't wish to see the crowd. Dear angel, I sent for my letters, and it pained me that among them there was not a word from thee, not a word in pencil, no good-evening. Dear lady, suffer me to love thee so much. When I can love any one more I will tell thee ; will leave thee un-plagued. Adieu, Gold. Thou understandst not how much I love thee."

Instead of one of his short, impromptu, im-passioned notes, he one day sends her the fol-lowing : —

"WANDERER'S NIGHT SONG.

" Thou who dost in Heaven bide,
　　Every pain and sorrow stillest,
　Him whom twofold woes betide
　　With a twofold solace fillest,
　Oh, this tossing, let it cease !
　　What means all this pain, unrest ?
　　　Soothing peace.
　　Come, oh come into my breast.
" *Feb.* 12, '76.　On the side of the Ettersberg."

This exquisite gem Charlotte showed to he. pious mother, who wrote on the back of it. " Peace I leave with you, my peace I give unto you : not as the world giveth, give I unto you.

Let not your heart be troubled, neither let it be afraid."

In Charlotte von Stein there was a supreme source of power and attraction ; she had what Madame de Sévigné thought was the high distinction of Madame de Lafayette, *une divine raison.* Strong proof it is of the substantial attractiveness of Charlotte, of a fine power in her, and at the same time of the moral resources of Goethe, that she was able to make a man such as Goethe was to be to her as a brother. Her success in elevating his love is shown in notes written on the twenty-third of February. The opening of the first note alludes evidently to a high discipline she had lately subjected him to : " How tranquilly and lightly I slept ; how happy I arose and greeted the beautiful sun, the first time for fourteen days with free heart, and with how much thanks to thee, angel of Heaven, to whom I owe it. I must say it to thee, thou only one among women who has given to my heart a love which makes me happy." And he cannot withold himself from writing to her again at midnight. I translate two sentences : " Thou only one whom I can love so much without being tormented by it ; and yet I live ever in fear. Would that my sister had one who would be to her a brother as thou art to me a sister."

Goethe knew himself when he wrote that he loved "ever in fear," that is, in fear of relapsing into the lower phase, out which Charlotte was doing her best to lift him. He did relapse more than once, as is proved by notes of different dates. Several weeks later he is in a great taking : " Wherefor should I wrong thee, dearest creature! Why deceive myself, and plague thee! We can be nothing to each other, and are too much. Good-night, dear angel, and good-morning. I will not see thee again — all that I could say is naught. Henceforth I will see thee as one sees the stars !"

Charlotte seems to have become sensitive to the talk of the world. "The world," that is, our neighbors, acquaintance, and "friends," will talk. And why should they not ? Every one complains of this inquisitive, inquisitorial talk as an impertinence. But has it not its good side ? Does it not often do the duty of a reminder to conscience ? The general conscience may, in some cases, be sounder than the individual. At times this over-curious analytic talk plays the part of an ubiquitous police, by whose irrepressible prying back alleys are kept the cleaner. In answer probably to warnings she had given him to be more distant and circumspect, the poor lover wails after this fashion :

"And so, this relation, the purest, truest, most beautiful, that I ever had with any woman except my sister, this, too, is to be broken up."

To Countess Stolberg, one of his confidential correspondents, whom he knew through her brothers, but had never seen, he had written, on the eighteenth of May about Charlotte: "I dined with the duke; after dinner I went to Frau von Stein, an angel of a woman, whom I have so often to thank for the becalming of my heart and for many of the purest blessings." Two days later he writes again to the countess about his sister, who is in trouble, begging her to write to his sister: "Oh, that you were in close friendship together! That in her loneliness a beam of light from thee shone upon her, and on the other hand that from her to thee there came in the hour of trouble a word of comfort. Become known to each other. Be to one another what I cannot be. Those who are true women should love no men: we are not worthy of it. Good-night — half-past ten." When he wrote those last two lines, was he not thinking of Charlotte?

VI.

WE have seen how, to the vexation and alarm
of the more sober personages, the machinery
of public affairs in the duchy got unscrewed
by the neglect and wild ways of the new young
sovereign ; and how the principal figure in the
little realm, after the duke, his consort Louise,
was ready to frown upon Goethe as the fascin-
ating tempter who misled her husband. The
young duchess could not yet value Goethe.
Even Charlotte, who withheld Louise from
blaming him, had not herself yet fully discerned what he was. It was, indeed, no easy
task to see into Goethe. Even to-day, many
clever, well-meaning people mistake him. The
first qualification for insight is sympathy. The
following extract from a letter of Charlotte to
her friend Zimmermann, shows that she had
misgivings as to Goethe's success in doing the
public work he had undertaken. Karl August
was the only one who divined what he was and

who trusted him entirely. The letter is dated the tenth of May, 1776: "Goethe is bringing about a great revolution here. If he can get things into order again, so much the better for his genius. 'T is certain that he has the best intentions, but too much youthfulness, and not enough experience. Let us await the result. All our good fortune here is vanished; since the beginning of the duke's reign our court is no more what it was. A prince, discontented with himself and with all the world, who is careless of his life, although he has little health to support it, a still less healthy brother, a dissatisfied mother, a discontented wife, — all good people, but who don't fit together."

In Goethe there was such a lively quantity and so high a quality of life that his mind was ever kept in productive motion, tending upwards. A man of genius, equipped with talents, as pliant instruments of genius, if he strikes into practical affairs about him, reanimates the common, and makes dull routine quiver with new organic vitality. The incapable, having in themselves no seeds of belief in original movement, being fit only to oil the old wheels, look on, stupefied, and cry out against spitting in the face of experience. One of the high functions of genius is to create fresh experience. In

what spirit Goethe entered upon his new career
we learn from a sentence of a letter to Lavater, so early as the sixth of March, 1776: "I
am now entirely embarked upon the billows of
the world, fully resolved to discover, to win, to
be ready for shipwreck or to blow myself with
the whole cargo into the air." This is giving lively epistolary expression to momentary
thoughts on the contingencies of the situation,
on imaginary dangers. No well proportioned
man, like Goethe, with such powers, but has a
consciousness of their sufficiency for whatever
he deliberately undertakes. How well he was
doing two months later, and how contented,
is seen in a letter to the Countess Stolberg:
"Could I describe to you my position here!
the most desirable, the most happy."

While, in the affairs of the court and duchy,
Goethe was bringing order out of confusion, he
was striving, by the requirement and help of
Charlotte, to tune his feelings towards her to a
higher key. The task she had imposed upon
him, and which he was trying to accomplish,
namely, to still the tumult of his heart, he found
harder than to subdue disorder in the ducal administration. During the summer he had a
trial from her absence in Pyrmont. He does
not seem, however, to have lost either sleep or

flesh. On the tenth of July he writes: " Last night I went to bed and was soon asleep; Philip brings me a letter; half awake I read — that Lilie is married!! turn over and go to sleep again. How I worship fate, that it deals so with me! Everything at the right time — dear angel, good-night." Here is a whole note. What bounding life in every line of it! "Only a word, best of women. My head is upside down, and I can say nothing. The day after to-morrow we go to Ilmenau, and would that you were in Kochberg. I miss you at all corners and terminations, and if you don't come back soon I shall do something foolish. At the bird-shooting in Apolda yesterday I fell in love with Christel von Artern. I have nothing to put me into a mild mood. Wieland does me most good. The duke and I share at least our stupor between us; everything else excites me, and I have not thee to fly to. Otherwise, it were not easy to find a happier being than I am, if I only had thee again. Oh, send me something. Greet Zimmermann."

After Charlotte's return he wrote her from Ilmenau: "Thy relation to me is so holy, so strange, that I feel it cannot be expressed in words; people cannot see it." And yet, a few days later, he seems to have borne himself in a way to profane this holiness ; for, on the sixteenth, in consequence of some check he had received, he writes : " I wish I could cease to trouble you with my unheavenly presence." She had occasionally still to forbid his coming to see her, as is shown by the following note of the eighth of September. " Yesterday I was out of spirits and know not why. I had a feeling that I should not see you to-day. I sent for the clarionet players, walked about in my garden ; they played until eight. It was all very fine, but my heart did not warm. Just as I was moving about in the morning comes your note. An hour before I had sent word to Wieland that I should like to see him ; it was from a presentiment that I should need some one. Adieu. I owe too much to fate to complain, and yet for my feelings I can do nothing. Adieu. I shall not go to Kochberg, for I understood word and look. Adieu." And worse than this ; not only would she not have him at Kochberg, but she begs him to send her Lenz (an eccentric friend of Goethe) to give her lessons in English. On the tenth he writes : " I send Lenz ; at last I have mastered myself enough to do it. Oh, you have a way of giving pain, like fate ; one cannot murmur, however much one suffers." From the tone of the rest of the note this looks only half serious. She was schooling him into good behavior, and he was cheerfully submitting to the discipline, she not afraid of losing her scholar, nor he of losing his teacher. He concludes as follows : "You will hear nothing further. I desire not to hear from you or Lenz. When anything is to be ordered, let him write to Philip (Goethe's servant)." . This was not sent until the third day, when he turned over the leaf and added : "Lenz will now go, and I had some scruple about sending you the foregoing page ; ah ! you can see how it often looks in my heart, how I can even become unjust to you. I thank you for the first remembrance from your writing-table, which I then did not hope to see again.[1] Yesterday I was at Belvidere (a suburban summer-palace). Louise (the duchess) is just an infinite angel ; I had to guard my eyes, that they did not gaze at her across the table — the gods will stand by us all. The Waldner (a maid of honor) is lovely ; I was with her early, we had much fooling. In the evening all the highnesses were at Tiefurt. Your husband was in fine mood, played comical tricks on the upper governess. I pitied the courtiers ; I

---

[1] Referring to his first visit to Kochberg soon after his arrival in Weimar, when he had yet no thought of remaining.

wonder that the most of them don't turn into
toads and snakes.

"Addio, my heart is still with you, dear, only
woman who makes me happy without making
me grieve — still not always without pain.
Ade, best one."

. In the late summer and early autumn Charlotte had two gratifications, — a visit from her
sister Imhoff, and the arrival of Herder.

In his high performances as reviver of the
affairs of Weimar, as infuser of new life into
institutions and administrations, Goethe made
no movement more serviceable than when he
prompted the duke to call Herder to Weimar,
as court-chaplain and ecclesiastical superin-
tendent. When Goethe was a student at
Strasburg he first met Herder, who was there
to consult a famous occulist. During a painful
surgical operation and tedious trying cure, to
which Herder had to submit, Goethe won his
heart by brotherly attention and tenderness.
Herder, only five years older than Goethe,
had then already a reputation as writer and
preacher. His father, usher of a female academy and leader of the choir of a church in
Morungen, East Prussia, was so poor that
young Herder had little early schooling, and,
like some other distinguished scholars and

writers, he owed his education and rapid di-
versified acquirement to an insatiable thirst for
knowledge. While studying at the university
of Koenigsberg, where Kant was a professor, he
supported himself by teaching. One of Herder's early literary efforts was an attempt to up-
set some positions of the great philosopher, a
task beyond his powers; for his mind had
neither the grasp nor the penetration of the
mighty metaphysician. Herder's mind was
more assimilative than original, more sympathetic than creative. His style is, like his
countenance, round, full, smooth, and graceful,
as was his bearing.

Goethe looked upon the meeting with Herder at Strasburg as one of his good fortunes.
To Herder, already launched upon the career
he was just entering, he owed enlargement of
his horizon and introduction to new spheres of
knowledge. "Few are as learned after the
same grand fashion as Herder," said Jean Paul
Richter. With all his occasional harshness, he
was a spiritually-minded aspiring man, and this
gave him a rare fitness for the pulpit. The
transearthly condition of man was almost a
vivid presence to him. He once told his friend
Richter that he had a strong wish to behold
an apparition, and had none of the usual fear
of a ghost.

To Weimar Herder was a great acquisition, another aristocrat added to that high circle of aristocrats. Louise and Charlotte enjoyed personal intercourse with him and valued his preaching, so superior to the generally dry dogmatism and shallow one-sidedness of the pulpit. And Goethe enjoyed him, and afterwards Schiller, although they, seeing the whole of him, were repelled from certain sides. Towards Goethe he always retained some of the feeling of ascendency, which, when they first met in Strasburg, had its appropriateness, — Goethe eager to learn from him, and he, with fame and wider knowledge, ready to impart to a willing learner, then an unknown law student. That this tone of mingled correction and patronage should have prolonged itself to the period when Goethe had surpassed him in fame and mental power, is partly pitiable, partly comical. It must have proceeded from a too strong feeling of his own worth, encouraged by that pretension to precedence entertained by the clerical profession toward their fellow-men, which is nursed by deference from the crowd of the ignorant and half educated.

Owing somewhat to the active feeling of self-approbation, which has the effect of shutting one too closely in one's self, Herder did not grow with years in the ratio that Goethe did. To unfold himself Goethe went out of himself; and the self being deep, and clear, and strong, the projection beyond it was far and wide and illuminated. He did not hug a self-seeking creed or self-flattering dogmas, thereby to narrow him; but he broadened himself by letting his heart move his head to ceaseless organic work, through the pen, embodying the feelings of his soul, through institutions and outward combinations embodying practical conceptions for the social and general weal.

On the dogmatic side Herder was less contracted than most of his professional brethren. But Goethe's field was not theological assumptions and convictions; his field was nature, and the divine principle everywhere exhibited by nature, and by man as the highest in nature. He could not rest in the man-made devices for strengthening and clarifying his soul; he sought to know the will that is ever active in the visible universe about him and the invisible universe within him; and being endowed with finest sensibilities and piercing, comprehensive intellect, in this lively search he grew to be one of the wisest of men and of the most serviceable to his fellows. In this high, active life, of twofold activity, of poetic med-

itation and performance and practical administrative achievement, an efficient ingredient was
self-forgetfulness. Only through a hushing of
the voice of self and listening to deeper, more
musical promptings, can a high level be reached
in any wide region of human endeavor.

VII.

SMOOTH WATER.

THE opening years of Charlotte had not been so fragrant with blossoms as to encourage hopes and enthusiasms, nor was her nature fiery enough to have fused in the warmth of an individual brain outside influences and pressures. Her destiny was, not to kindle new flames in the world, but, through the power of moral feeling and feminine purity, conjoined with feminine fascination, to temper and chasten and regulate at the outset the fire of the most creative mind of the age, and by spiritual control give steadier movement to his great powers. The effects of the exertion of this unique privilege, already apparent in the first year of his residence in Weimar, were more distinct in the second.

Goethe, running over with spontaneity and animal life, and of amorous temperament, was especially open to female charm. In his youth and earliest manhood he seems to have been saved from injurious or imprudent connections

6

by power of self-control, an ingredient in which was sense of duty and propriety, and by invisible guardianship. He arrived in Weimar prepared to admire Charlotte, and intercourse with her soon converted admiration into a deeper feeling. When Charlotte sought to lift him to her higher plane, Goethe did not draw off from her and attach him to less conscientious dames, who would be willing in his favor to suspend their marital duties. That he did not do this exhibits the elevation of his nature, and that he was capable of the refined sympathy which Charlotte required for the purer union with her. Had Goethe, with all his sensuousness, not been, at the same time, susceptible to the nobler attraction, he would soon have ceased his intimacy with Charlotte. His love for her, spiritualized by her, held him for ten years.

In the second year a change of tone is perceptible in his notes. Passionate outbreaks occur hardly at all, the intimate *du* is seldom used. At the same time the intimacy deepens, and roots itself in mutual small kindnesses: out of his garden he sends asparagus, flowers, begs of her something for a meal, invites himself to dine with her, tells stories to her children in the evening, summons them to his garden-house to see fireworks, and, owing to a storm, keeps the youngest all night. Here is a note writen towards the end of February, 1777 : " I have advised the duke to dine with you to-day : he is not in the best spirits. If you will have us, we will come towards one. But don't have any formality. Herewith I send old wine. Addio." The unceremoniousness, the primitive (wholesome) hour of one, the, at times, willful Karl August, hardly twenty-one, and she (look at her face) seated between such two. What a picture ! and what the talk must have been, — Goethe moved to his best by her presence, and the duke, shaken out of his low spirits by such neighbors ; and she, proud of them both, loving them both ; and the old Rhenish, quaffed from pale straw-colored or light green generous bulbous glasses. Will not some sympathetic artist make a triple portrait of the rare scene ? What a light he might throw into the meaningful countenance of Charlotte as she catches a stroke of Goethe's most genial young wisdom.

On the sixteenth of June Goethe writes to Charlotte in Kochberg : " At eight I was in my garden, found everything doing well, and walked up and down reading. At nine I receive a letter that my sister is dead. I can say nothing further." This, his only sister, had

been, especially in boyish days, very dear to
Goethe. For consolation he went out to Kochberg. Soon afterwards Charlotte betook herself to Pyrmont, whither her husband had
gone for his health. In her absence Goethe
goes again to Kochberg, and in a letter reminds
her that a year ago she had forbidden him to
come thither. On the seventh of July he
writes from Weimar : " I have received your
note ; I guessed its contents, and this was the
first time I ever had an unwillingness to open
a note from you. What can I say to you !
Farewell." This was probably the announcement of the death of her little daughter. A
few days later he writes her from " Kochberg,
Saturday the twelfth July, early eight. This
week I did not feel comfortable in the town, and
yesterday I took flight, setting out on foot from
Weimar at half-past five in the afternoon, and
reached this at half-past nine, where all was
already locked up, and the inmates were getting ready for bed. On my shouting I was first
recognized by old Dorothea and by her and the
cook welcomed with loud cries. Kaestner [the
tutor] then came down with his pipe, and
Karl, who the whole day had maintained that I
would come. Ernest, who was in his shirt but
dressed himself. Fritz was already asleep. I

drank a quantity of Zelzer water, we told our doings of the week, and the drawings were produced."

At this period Goethe wasted much time in drawing after nature, not having discovered apparently until he got to Rome that in pictorial art he never could exceed mediocrity. In his notes to Charlotte frequent mention is made of hours spent in drawing.

Between Charlotte and the Duchess Louise there was a cordial attachment, strengthened and perpetuated by mutual esteem. On Charlotte's writting to her from Pyrmont of the gain to her husband's health, Louise acknowledged the letter on the twenty-fifth July from Belvidere. This letter discloses the intimate relation existing between the subject of our memoir and the highest "lady of the land," and is further valuable as giving the reader a glance into other relations among the topmost personages of Weimar : —

"A thousand thanks for your letter, my dear Stein. Believe me that it has given me a great pleasure. The news you give me of the restoration of your husband has afforded me a genuine joy. The weather is little favorable to me ; scarcely can I go out of the house ; that depresses me. The day before yesterday I was at Ettersburg,[1] and I was wearied to death. I assure you always I dread going thither, although the mood of my very dear mother-in-law is a little better than in your time. She is furious that Herder preached in Pyrmont, I know not wherefore. As regards me in Belvidere, I trouble myself little about the human race, and could wish that it troubled itself little about me. Werther is back, but shuts herself up in Frohndorf. For some days past the duke has been in the sulks with me, and I know not wherefore, but I take it very quietly. How does your English get on? I have forgotten the little that I knew, but next winter I shall take to it again. Say much from me to your husband and to Herder. If my niece Charlotte is still in Pyrmont, give her a thousand greetings from me. Is the crown-prince of Brunswick towards you what he was last year? Farewell, my dear Stein! I love you with all my heart; be assured of this. Your true friend Louise. Come back soon, and don't bury yourself in Kochberg."

On the eleventh of August Goethe sends her, inclosed in the following note, some stanzas addressed to her, part written by the duke and part by himself : " That I ever dreamily nourish

---

[1] Residence of the Dowager Duchess Amalia.

myself on the phenomena of nature and on my love for you, you see from the accompanying. I must hold steadfast, otherwise your sorrow would carry me away ; and it afflicts me so much, that I am obliged often to keep myself from dwelling on the only thing that is left to my heart, — your image." Writing to take leave on the twenty-seventh, before starting for Eisenach, he begs of her to think of him on the morrow, his birthday. But on the way to Eisenach he could not keep himself from making a *détour* by Kochberg, where he surprised her on his birthday. On the twenty-ninth he continued his journey towards Eisenach, and in the evening writes from Manebach: " Best angel, you gave me provisions for the journey. God know hows I shall be flayed in Eisenach ; I go in the dark to meet my fate, and let not my imagination make it better or worse." He was going as companion to the duke, who liked hunting much more than Goethe did. He lodged in the Wartburg, and describes to Charlotte what a glorious lodging it is, with its far outlook over mountain and meadow, up at glittering cliffs and down into gorges. Goethe had the faculty of working while on a journey or away from home ; and so, while the duke and the others were busy with wild boars, he sat in the high solitude of his castle and gave himself up to prolific meditation or to delightful production. In the second week of September he informs Charlotte that he has "invented a wild thing, a comic opera, 'Die Empfindsamen' (Sentimental People) as mad and rough as possible. If Seckendorf will set it to music, it can be played this winter. I have begun to dictate to Philip." The faithful Philip, whom he had brought with him from Frankfort, was both secretary and servant. On the evening of the thirteenth September he exclaims : " Here I now dwell, dearest, and sing psalms to the Lord, who out of pains and narrowness has brought me to elevation and grandeur. The duke caused me to move up here. · With the people below, who may be very good people, I have nothing in common, nor they with me ; some of them imagine they love me, but it is not so."

Goethe's fears of being bored at Eisenach turned out imaginary. The Wartburg and his own soul saved him. If, instead of egotistically devising contrivances for saving their souls, people would set their souls to saving them, they would find themselves better off. He enjoyed one of the richest possible phases of human activity, that of creative literary work, — a phase that is rich and happy, because some of the best faculties are in eager combined pursuit of fresh game poetically started. Besides the comic opera, he wrote several lyrical poems. At the end of September he had the further enjoyment of a week's visit from Merck. Even when he had to work at tasks that were irksome, or to interchange with people not to his taste or of his way of being, he was thereby ripening his powers, drawing profit out of the seemingly unprofitable, such assimilative, joined to such selective, virtue was there in his mind. From a note to Charlotte on the sixteenth September I take a short passage: " Your blessing has been fulfilled ; Eisenach and the wild boars have not flayed me. I see every day more distinctly that in this quagmire we have to suffer more or less. Write me something about the children and Peter."

On the seventh of November he writes from Weimar: " To-day it is just two years since I came hither. To live these over again ! ? ? — To take in with one look the morning that I first waked in Weimar, two years ago, up to to-day, is most strange to me, at once gladsome and affecting. How much has fate given me, and by degrees, as we deal delights to children, so that I enjoyed each good fully as it came and made it my own, and thus I have been lovingly initiated into feelings and circumstances which before were most remote from me."

One of the privileges it is of the poetical organization to play with its own sensations, to stand aloof from them, so that they being, by this high power of abstraction and self-disintegration, converted, for the moment, into objective phenomena, they are addressed as such and questioned whether they be illusions or realities. In this mood Goethe writes the next day: " Yesterday, on leaving you, I had wondrous thoughts, among others, — whether I really love you, or whether your presence delights me like that of a very clear looking-glass, which mirrors one's self so distinctly."

One day, towards the end of November, Goethe, out on a hunting party at Eisenach with the duke, left his companions, saying he would rejoin them later. He then rode on to the Hartz Mountains, a ride secretly planned. In this excursion he had a threefold purpose ; to behold the mountain region in winter, to examine the mines, with a view to his design of reviving those of Ilmenau, and to have an interview with a Wertherian young man who had twice written to him for counsel. Goethe, more than most men, needed occasional change, to get refreshment and enlargement by the shifting of scenes and conditions. He was ever seeking renewal of power at fresh fountains of nature. A winter ascent of the Brocken would be an invigorating bath to his mind, a letting in of heaven upon faculties long pent in circles of earthly anxieties.

What the success was of the undertaking may be judged from the opening of a note to Charlotte on the second of December: "The joy that I have as a child, you should be able to see in a mirror! How true that nothing is wonderful but the natural, and nothing great but the natural, and nothing, etc., etc., etc., but the natural! ! ! ! ! To-day I sat on a crag —you should see it — where neither gods nor men would have looked for me."

Students of Goethe know the depth of his humanity, and how from this depth come up lights that sparkle on the surface of his pages and make their chief attraction, like stars on the expanse of heaven, which, while seemingly on the surface, lie far in the unfathomable blue, and give it its power and beauty and significance. Goethe's love for and sympathy with his fellows was the inspiriting virtue of his rich nature, the soul of his poetry and his art. After having been among the forges and foundries, he writes from Goslar on the fourth December : " Here am I again buried among the walls and roofs of antiquity.   I have a host who is quite fatherly ; there is so much fine homeliness in the house that one is very comfortable.   On this dark expedition how much love do I again feel for that class of people called the lower ! but which for God is assuredly the highest.   For among them are all the virtues together, — moderation, contentedness, straightforwardness, fidelity, rejoicing over the least good, harmlessness, patience, perseverance in un — un — I will not lose myself in exclamations. . . . . I am now drying my things ! they are hung around the stove. How little man needs, and how pleasant it is when he feels how *much* he needs that little. When in future you make me a present, let it be something that will be useful on such a journey."

He traveled on this occasion under an assumed name, and thus describes the effect on himself : " It gives me a strange sensation to move about in the world unknown.   It is as though my relation to men and things was much more truly felt by me.   I am called

Weber, am a painter, have studied law, or a mere traveler, bear myself politely towards every one, and am everywhere well received. With women have I as yet had nothing to do. A complete calm and security enfolds me ; so far everything has turned out fortunately ; the sky grows clearer, it will freeze hard to-night." On the seventh he sends an extract from his diary: "Homesickness. To Klausthal. Strange sensation, out of the imperial city [Goslar], which with and in its privileges is crumbling, to come up here where from subterranean blessing [the mines] the mountain towns joyfully grow. Birthday of my departed sister." Here is part of a note written on the same day in the evening : "The best of this pilgrimage is that at every step I find confirmed my ideas on administration, be it of a peasant's farm or a principality, and that they are so simple that one needed not to travel if one could learn something by one's self. Only the loneliness I can't get used to ; I did better formerly, you have spoilt me ; many an hour I long to be at home again." And here, two days later, is a sample of that wisdom which gives to Goethe's pages such solid attractiveness. Never was there a man who saw more distinctly surfaces and at the same time what is

beneath them: "In my disguise I see every
day how easy it is to be a rogue, and what an
advantage over the egoism of people that man
gains who practices self-denial." His dearest
wish, and the most importunate motive for the
excursion into the Hartz Mountains was to ascend to the top of the Brocken in winter ; and
that, in the teeth of warnings from the
dwellers in the mountains, during the week,
he accomplished, accompanied by the warden
of the forest, who an hour before had pronounced the attempt rash, but who was probably overcome by the magnetic enthusiasm of
the unknown traveler. Starting at a quarter
past ten, they reached the summit in three
hours, being blessed with full sunlight on the
top while all below lay under clouds.

VIII.

AN EPISODE.

HAD Charlotte von Stein never met Goethe, I should not now be endeavoring to write a memoir of her, out of the endeavor drawing a high enjoyment, and with the hope that there will be readers to share in it. In this she is only in the same position as Weimar and all that it contains. The squares and walks of the quiet little capital are consecrated ground, which the pilgrim treads with the visionary consciousness of a majestic invisible presence, because for a half century they were familiar with the footsteps of the foremost genius of Germany, and for many years with those of his great compeers. Two of these became residents of Weimar on Goethe's motion. Wieland he found there, but it was his creative influence that drew thither first Herder and afterwards Schiller.

If Charlotte owes to Goethe the perpetuation of her name, Weimar possibly owes to Charlotte that Goethe's autumnal visit in 1775 grew into a life-long residence. Goethe was attracted to the young duke, who at the age of nineteen gave tokens of manhood in judgment as well as in character; and the fascination which Goethe made all feel who at that period came within the sphere of his personal action, was, over the duke, an irresistible sway, a sway exerted purely for good. Karl August was impetuous, sometimes willful, and occasionally rough. Goethe saw through the outward and temporary into the core of a character, and soon got to love and esteem his young friend and admirer. But whether Karl August and his court, even with Louise and Wieland and Amalia, would have had the attrahent force to make him enter upon a new mode of life, opposite to any his imagination had ever pictured to him, this may be questioned; and, considering the qualities of the man, it may be believed that Charlotte was the anchor that held him to Weimar and made him look upon it as a home.

"The eternal womanly" lay deep in the soul of Goethe, else he never would or could have brought it into prominence so significantly at the end of the second part of "Faust," nor could he have given buoyant life to so many various female figures in his poems. The power of woman over him was unusually strong.

Hence Charlotte became his "confessor, adviser, soother." The woman who could be that to Goethe during ten years of his early, fiery, teeming manhood, has thereby crowned herself with a unique wreath which a long posterity will delight to recognize and admire. Women of ordinary mental endowment sometimes, through personal beauty and art, captivate superior men ; but in such cases the captivation is sensuous and temporary. Here was a woman who, for a decade, commanded the exclusive devotion of a warm, sensuous man, a preëminent genius, and seven years younger than herself. That which wrought such unusual effect was the power of moral self-command, wielded by a woman possessed of those fine intuitions which are the fruit of marriage between a clear reason and unbribed sensibilities ; to these were superadded womanly dignity and grace. On his part active sympathy with woman was conjoined with capacity for appreciating what in her is highest and best, and thus his whole being surrendered itself to the delightful and chastening dominion of Charlotte.

Whatever of beauty and of joy there is in life is due to love. From love, in its manifold movements and frank impulsions, come all harmonies, all excellences. A perpetual renovator,

7

an untiring reconciler, an hourly elevator, love
is the central force of being. Only its abuses
are harmful. Goethe was a rarely lovable
man. All who came into intercourse with him
loved him, men, women, children. Charlotte
was one of his lovers, a privileged lover ; for it
was her high distinction to bind their love with
the bonds of duty and to withhold it from in-
continent aberration. The noble, womanly
function of refiner and purifier never woman
had such opportunity to perform, never with
better and wider results. By the cheer of her
sympathy she comforted the man in his con-
flicts with vexatious affairs and prosaic people ;
by the softer play of her intellect she threw acceptable light upon the poet's ideal endeavors.
She was a bridge between him and much that
was distasteful to him. During those crowded
ten years of his life she enlivened and elevated
his moods, she stimulated the productiveness
of his genius. Amid the halfnesses, the insin-
cerities, the incompetencies which impede and
chafe a superior man, variously in contact with
others, what a refreshment to have so clear,
strong, susceptive a nature as Charlotte von
Stein to resort to when the work of the day
was done. For ten years her house was a
haven of recruitment and rest to the most

active, the most earnest, the most genial of
men.

In these years their feelings and thoughts
were so interwoven that what relates to Goethe
concerns Charlotte. To her he confided his
joys and his troubles. He read Shakespeare
to her, and his own poems, fresh from their
mysterious womb, and "Wilhelm Meister," as
the earlier chapters were written. That she
should be a medium for imparting minuter and
very precious knowledge of Goethe is a glory
she has finely earned. Through an intimate
relation, as honorable to her as it was serviceable to him, her name is forever linked to his.
From his countless notes to her, written often
with pencil, we learn what that relation was,
and what a charm and what a good it was to
him. The last that have been quoted were
from the Hartz Mountains. Before quitting
the year 1777, it will be in place here to relate
the issue of one of his purposes in visiting the
Hartz, that of having an interview with his unknown Wertherian correspondent. This he
related to Charlotte on his return from the expedition, and he has given, with his wonted circumstantiality and distinctness, an account of
it at the end of his history of the campaign
in France in 1792.

"Werther," by many supposed to be the cause of much moral derangement among the youth of Germany, towards the close of the last century, was itself but one effect of that derangement, — the passionate expression thereof through the voice of a brilliant genius, himself a sufferer from the psychic epidemic. The sudden immense vogue of " Werther" arose from its aptness and timeliness as such expression. It was a match suddenly flaring in the midst of accumulated combustibles. Goethe had to bear the charge of being the source of that whereof he was the most conspicuous product. Thence the author of " Werther" received numerous applications for spiritual help from unhealthily sentimental young people, who were, or fancied themselves to be, suffering Werthers. One of these lived at Wernigerode, in the Hartz Mountains.

In 1776 Goethe received from Wernigerode a very long letter, in which, through much genuine feeling, was discernible at bottom willfulness instead of endurance, more stubbornness than fortitude. The plaintive outpouring, well-written, as if by a young man educated for the pulpit or a professorship, was, upon the whole, not of a character to move much sympathy or hope. Nevertheless, Goethe felt that if he could see the writer face to face, he might perhaps be of service to him; but he was deterred from inviting him to an interview by the unsuccessful termination of several similar cases. He therefore took no notice of the letter. This silence evoked a second, not so long as the first, but more passionate and urgent. Nor to the second did Goethe make any reply; but a year later, one of his motives for a visit to the Hartz Mountains was the desire to talk face to face with this correspondent.

Arriving early in December at Wernigerode, which lies at the foot of the Brocken, he inquired of an intelligent waiter at the inn if there were not in the town any educated young men who would like to receive a visit from a traveling stranger. The first whom the waiter mentioned was Plessing. This being the name of Goethe's correspondent, he sent to inquire whether a visit from an artist would be agreeable to him; and receiving at once a favorable answer, he was shown to the house about dusk and was kindly received, giving himself out as a painter from Gotha. Hereupon Plessing eagerly said that living so near to Weimar he must have been there, and probably knew some of the distinguished men of that city; to which Goethe replied affirmatively, mentioning several of them. "But you don't mention Goethe," exclaimed Plessing, impatiently. I know him, too, said the sham painter, and have met him in the company of the others, but he lives much alone. Plessing, who had listened with restless attention, now broke in with excitement, begging to have a description of the man who had made himself so talked of. Hereupon Goethe ingenuously described himself; and had his questioner been more calm, with some power of insight, he could not have failed to suspect that Goethe himself was before him.

Plessing had risen and was walking up and down the room. He ordered refreshment and wine, poured out for his guest and himself, emptied his own glass at a single draught, seized Goethe's arm, saying with great excitement: "Excuse my extraordinary conduct, but you inspire me with so much confidence that I must reveal all to you. This man, such as you describe him, ought at any rate to have answered me. I sent him a circumstantial, cordial letter, I depicted to him my condition, my sufferings, begged him to interest himself in me, to advise me, to help me; and now many months are passed and I hear nothing from him; at least, after such unbounded trust, I deserved a word declining my request."

To this his visitor answered that he was unable either to explain or to excuse such conduct ; so much, however, he knew from personal experience, that on this well-disposed, well-wishing, kindly young man there was such an incumbent pressure from ideal as well as from real things, that it was often out of his power to move, let alone to act. " As we are got so far," said Plessing, with some composure, " I must read to you the letter, and you shall judge for yourself whether it did not deserve some acknowledgment."

To a penetrating, clear observer, like Goethe, there was a philosophic satisfaction in again recognizing how a living creature in all its movement and conduct is ever in harmony with itself. The reader fitted perfectly the written text, but he took no deeper hold of Goethe's feeling than the letter itself had taken when received in Weimar. The earnestness of the young man could not but interest his listener ; but, although the tenderer feelings were involved, there was no charm in his delivery, and a contracted egoism was very transparent. When he had finished he asked Goethe with quickness what he had to say now, and whether such an appeal did not deserve, nay, demand, an answer.

The reading had made only more evident the unhappy condition of the young man. He was one who had never taken any note of the outward world, but had read much, and having turned all his thoughts and power inward, had done himself much harm in this way, as in the depths of his being there was no productive talent.

Having, continues Goethe, learnt from happy experience in myself and others that in such cases a vigorous, trustful recourse to nature and her boundless manifold affluence is the best remedy, I determined, after some reflection, to try it here, and said to him that I thought I understood "why the young man (Goethe) in whom you have placed so much confidence has remained silent; for his present way of thinking differs so widely from yours that he could not hope that you and he would understand each other. I have myself been present at conversations in that circle when it was maintained that one could be lifted out of a painful, self-torturing, gloomy state of mind only by active, hearty participation in the ongoings of the outward world. The most general acquaintance with nature, no matter on which side, a lively taking hold, either as gardener, or cultivator, or hunter, or miner, draws us away from ourselves ; that the applying of the intellectual powers to real sure phenomena produces by degrees the greatest comfort, clearness and instruction."

The young man grew restless and impatient ; notwithstanding which, his guest went on in the same tone, relating how his own devotion to nature, as landscape-painter, made him take delight in all her aspects and at the same time tended to the unfolding and cultivating of his inward powers. With poetic glow he described the enjoyment he had even in this winter journey to the mountains, depicting the variegated appearances caused by sunlight on cliff and snowy summit and frosted gorge, the play of light from the guide's lantern upon water, especially the effect on him of the famous cave. Here his host interrupted him sharply, assuring him that he always regretted having visited the cave, which had not at all come up to the picture formed of it in his mind. These morbid symptoms did not take Goethe by surprise ; for, how often, he adds, had he occasion to observe that people fail to perceive the value of a bright reality, preferring to it some dark phantom of their own gloomy imagination. As little was he surprised when, on asking what image had been formed of the cave before seeing it,

Plessing gave a description which " the boldest
scene-painter of a theater would scarcely have
ventured to present as the vestibule to the Plu-
tonian regions."

A further attempt to put the despondent man
on a more cheerful and a safer track was met
by such decided negation, that Goethe, who had
come with the best intentions, felt himself ab-
solved from all further duty towards the sufferer. It was now late, and when Plessing
wished to read the second, more excited letter,
his visitor excused himself on account of the
day's fatigue. Plessing then invited him very
urgently to dinner the following day, an answer
to which invitation Goethe begged to postpone
until early the next morning. And so they
parted in the most friendly manner. This
young man was of medium size ; his features
had in them nothing attractive, nor were they
repulsive, and his soured condition did not
make him discourteous.

Stepping into the air, Goethe beheld "the
whole heaven sparkling with stars, streets and
squares covered with snow. I stood still upon
a foot-bridge and contemplated the wintry
world by night. I thought, too, of the adventure, and determined not to see the young man
again ; I therefore ordered my horse to be ready

by day-break, gave a note of apology for Plessing to the waiter who-had made me acquainted
with the young man, of whom I spoke good
words, of which, doubtless, the waiter made his
own use."

For some years Goethe heard nothing from
the sufferer, when one morning he announced
himself by a note as being in Weimar, to which
Goethe answered that he should be glad to see
him. Goethe expected a surprise, but Plessing
entered quietly and said : " I am not astonished
to find you here : the handwriting of your note
brought so distinctly to my memory the one
you wrote me on leaving Wernigerode that I
felt sure that I should find here that mysterious traveler." They then had a friendly talk
in the old strain, and, after several interviews,
parted on good terms, only that Goethe could
not reciprocate Plessing's desire for an intimate
union of friendship. For some time they cor-
responded, and Goethe had it in his power to
do him some good turns, for which Plessing
was becomingly grateful. His letters were always full of himself. He gained some name
as a writer of books on the older philosophy,
especially that which leaned to the mysterious.

Fifteen years after his visit to the Hartz,
Goethe, returning from the campaign in France,

went to see Plessing in Duisburg on the lower
Rhine, where he was professor in the University. He was not in very prosperous circumstances, and had ruined his health by severe
indoor study; nor had he yet found any so-
lution to his gloomy psychic problems, and
seemed ever striving after the unattainable.

The chief trouble with Plessing was a common one among men, the very prevalent trouble,
— egoism. He dwelt in himself with such inward delight that other delights were insipid to
him. He hugged the self as the drunkard hugs
the low desire which is his ruin. In Plessing,
as in so many others, the aggregate of qualities
that make up the self being but faintly lighted
by the higher attributes of humanity, — which
are ever urging us out of ourselves, — the persistent clinging to what was most active in him
darkened and enslaved his mind instead of il-
lumining and liberating it. There was thus
nothing in him to respond to the broad appeals
of Goethe who, through the vivifying interest
in nature which carried him to the top of the
Brocken in winter, not only practiced what he
preached, but who enjoyed a higher objectivity
even than this when he sought a fellow-suf-
ferer in order to comfort and enlighten him,
and who made the doing for others one of the
daily motors of his life.

By intense subjectivity, by centering upon self all one's thoughts and wishes, many a man becomes a curse to himself. So beautifully are we constituted that the greatest good to ourselves can only be reaped from the good of our fellows, and contributions thereto are our sole valid tickets of admission to the elysiums of life, to fullest enjoyment of being. Egoism is far from always taking the form of despondency, of gloomy restlessness, as with Plessing. In him probably a native hopelessness was aggravated by a semi-conscious incapacity to attain certain aims ; but no man whose motto is the Dutch proverb, *zelf is de man*, can be cheerful, whatever superficial flutter of gayety may sometimes enliven his exterior ; and the depth of the inward gloom is measured by the enormity of the egoism.

IX.

Is any other people but the German so fond
of beer as to make of it a soup? In Germany
this preparation is so acceptable that it is related of Goethe and the duke, that they one
day made a dinner on beer-soup. It came
about probably in this wise: the sovereign and
his minister, working together at Goethe's garden-house, were surprised by the dinner hour,
and sat down contentedly to the national soup;
as I did once myself when, visiting a distinguished German poet, I was cordially invited to
stay to dinner, where the principal dish was
beer-soup. I must say, that had the dinner
been of more account to me than the company,
— the poet and his wife, — I should have been
much disappointed.

Notwithstanding that Goethe could, and did,
at times — it may have been often — dispose of
a bottle of Rhenish at dinner, he was habitually frugal. He speaks of the necessity of an
abstemious diet when in a productive mood, a

necessity whereof all genial workers, nay, all head-workers, have repeated unmistakable experience. Here is a note to Charlotte, February 11, 1778, which is another witness to the frugality of his table: "I feel to-day that I must again remain hidden. My kitchen gives me nothing but pease and sausage.; after twelve I shall send to you for an addition. It seems to me as though a change were going on in me, but I cannot yet interpret it." This, no doubt, refers to one of those exalted mental states when the faculties seem to be in prophetic agitation, when there comes, one knows not whence, a fresh influx of creative vitality, disclosing new channels, of easy entrance, giving to the poetic soul clearer consciousness of spiritual life, and making it feel potent for any achievement. From within itself, apparently, the mysterious center of thought and emotion is flooded with waves of light, that open rapturous glimpses into life and nature and promise great solutions.

In a sentence at the end of a note, written a few days later, is another indication of Goethe's self-control in diet: "We had good fooling yesterday and slept long to-day; I abstained from punch and wine in the evening, and know my part very well." This refers to a private theatrical performance.

In May of 1778 Goethe accompanied Karl
August on a visit to Berlin. How proud must
have been the young duke to show his poet-
minister to the royalties and grandees of the
Prussian capital. Potsdam and Berlin were
then bristling with the energies of coming war.
This had interest for Goethe, always watchfully
awake to the activities of life, in whatever
form ; and this was a new spectacle. But the
crowd of dignitaries and court officials at Berlin, with its formal shows and glittering surface, its hollowness and pretension, was distasteful to him, a lover of the natural and the
substantial. Goethe, in his many-sidedness, was
a graceful man of the world, and could play his
part becomingly in unavoidable externalities ;
but his mind, craving ever nutrition, found no
satisfaction in the aridities of superficial intercourse. There are people, and some of them
not without mental calibre, who find enjoyment
in whirling from month to month through the
monotonous rounds of social entertainment,
who, living largely on surfaces, touch surfaces
with surfaces, are afraid of depths, prefer shal-
lows, like commonplace varnished better than
genius, enjoy the conventional more than the
true, the transitory more than the everlasting,
upholstery more than art. Goethe was not one

of these. He sought ever to inform social converse with intellect, to enliven and elevate it with the inventions of literature and· art. His example and his authority have done much to improve the tone of " society" in Germany.

On the seventeenth of May he writes to Charlotte. from Berlin : " It is a fine feeling to sit beside the fountain of war at the very moment when it threatens to gush forth. And the pomp and pride of the royal city, and the life and order and overflow, which were naught without the thousands upon thousands of men willing to be sacrificed. Men, horses, carriages, artillery, armaments, — it swarms with them." How his human sympathy and insight waft him on a flash into the core of the portentous spectacle, and seize upon the sublime central heat that gives life to the whole, — the readiness of men to die for a cause or their country.

Two days later he writes from Berlin in another vein : " If on my return I only could describe all to you : if I only dared to. But ah ! the iron cords that inclose my heart fasten themselves more tightly every day, so that at last nothing will flow through. If you wish to continue the figure, there lies fine allegory in it.

" So much I can say, the bigger the world

8

the more hideous is the farce, and I swear, no coarseness and foolery of buffoons is more disgusting than the bustling interaction of the upper and the lower middle classes. I pray the gods to enable me to preserve my courage and uprightness to the end, and rather hasten the end than let me creep meanly through the last part of my undertaking. But the value which this adventure, as further experience, has for me, for us all, is not to be named."

From Potsdam he writes on the twenty-first of May : "I have purified my soul by a sound sleep. We came back here yesterday evening. We wish to look round here again : my longing is, forward, towards home."

Poets are liable to color a statement more highly than the naked fact demands. Without overstepping the modesty of nature, their prose-diction at times blows into poetic ripeness. Goethe seems to have been moved by this warmth in the second letter from Berlin. His experience of two years, as zealous administrative foreman of the Duchy of Weimar, had not given him hope of doing much deep good. He was somewhat disappointed, and the sight of the ongoings in a large city, of the systematic selfishness, the preying of class upon class, of man upon man, turned, for the moment, his disappointment into despair, to which he here gave intimate vivacious expression. A strong understanding, with clear method, insight into character, and a close realistic grasp, empowered Goethe to be a practical statesman ; but while he was the competent counselor of the duke, and his active right hand, his ideal tendencies, especially at times of political miscarriage, were constantly floating him away from prosaic duties, and making him long for more literary leisure. This letter is, apparently, an utterance of such discontent.

Humane as he was, and, through his own gifts, intuitively cognizant of human nature, Goethe did not take what may be called a deeply scientific view of man and his social and moral capabilities, and thence, he did not distinctly perceive that vices and crimes are not an inherent necessity of human condition, but are only a relative result, the effect of passions perverted, — passions which, if working in wise combination, may make that bloom which now they blast. In several places, especially towards the end of the second part of "Wilhelm Meister," Goethe shows that he had a perception of the virtue there is in the associative principle, but not a perception penetrating enough to discern that in this principle, — to which is due civilization and human advancement,—there is latent a power to harmonize the discords of industry and social union, and so to vivify all man's multifarious work that the present semi-chaos shall shape itself into beneficent order.

A letter, written by Goethe to Lavater, in August, 1780, finds here a fitting place. Its spirit is the opposite to the despondency of the Berlin letter to Charlotte. As expressing consciousness of great powers, and a noble aspiration this letter is most significant, and it is otherwise valuable : —

"Ostheim, *August*, 1780.

"I only received to-day thy two letters of the second and ninth of this month. We have been into some remote bailiwicks of the Principality Eisenach to see several new, good, and useful undertakings which have been started since last spring.

"The task that is laid on me, that every day grows lighter and heavier, requires my presence, waking and dreaming. This duty becomes daily dearer to me, and in performing it I would wish to do like the greatest men. This desire to carry into the air as high as possible the point of the pyramid of my existence, whose basis is already designed and founded, outweighs all else, and is hardly for a moment forgotten. I dare not delay, I am already far forward in years [he was then thirty-one!] and perhaps fate will break me in the middle, and the Babylonian tower remain obtuse and unfinished. At least men shall say it was boldly projected, and if I live, the resources, God willing, shall suffice to reach the top.

" Much, too, is done by the charm of a beautiful love with which Frau von Stein seasons my life. One after the other she has inherited my mother, sister, and all the women I have loved ; and there has been woven a bond like the bonds of nature.

" Adieu, dearest ; remain near to me in spirit. With the Dürers, which are late, come flowers and bunches of plants which I gather on the road. Let only a few see them [probably comments on heads by Dürer] and no pretentious authors ; the rascals have ever copied and imitated me, and made my manner ridiculous and to stink in the nostrils of the public. Write me what you think of them.

" I await thy judgment ; thy alterations will be a subject of discussion between us and a study of genuine criticism.

" Herder continues to make his own life and that of others uncomfortable.

" The duke is very good and honest. If I could only get from the gods some more expansiveness for him. The chains by which the spirits lead us, press some of his limbs too tightly, while in others he has the fullest freedom.

" Since I have given up all physiognomical pretensions, my perception has grown very keen and enjoyable, I know almost in the first minute what to think of people.

" In physiognomy some leading points are become clear, which to thee doubtless have long been plain, which to me are however important on account of their consequences.

" Have I already described to you the saying *Individuum est ineffabile*, out of which I deduce a whole world ?

" It is all right as to the Bodm. manuscript. Greet B. and thy wife.   G."

In the spring of 1779 Goethe felt moved to lift into verse his " Iphigenia," which had been first written in prose. The influence of Charlotte in deepening and elevating his conception of woman is clearly traceable in the character of Iphigenia, one of the most human, majestic, and beautiful figures that ever issued from a poet's brain. To the poet's warm in-

timacy with Frau von Stein are owing some
of the finer elements of the Grecian princess's
individuality. On this point Schöll, the competent editor of Goethe's letters to Frau von
Stein, in the preface to those of 1779, speaks
thus admirably : " That was a new spring of the
soul, in which grew up in the poet, *Iphigenia*,
a poem whose whole substance is soul. Here
the light of the poem is a womanly soul, child-
like and wise, open and unapproachable, sympathetic and pure ; as in *Tasso* there breathes the
bloom of poetry in the figure of the princess
with her noble tender nature. In no other
earlier or later work has Goethe glorified womanly worth with so ethereal, one might say,
so youthful a devotion, as in these two works.
In the one, the sober, gentle priestess, secure
in the purity of nature, who restrains and di-
rects to good the advances of her friend, heals
the sick spirit of her brother, and through
clearness of soul reconciles contending men
and conflicting duties. In the other, a woman
purified by suffering, who with self-renuncia-
tion and tender wisdom loves the poet, con-
trols and yet cannot subdue him. The elements for both we find in the few past years
of Goethe's life, when we call to mind his
inward struggles."

Düntzer, who, in order to execute the *Life picture* of Frau von Stein, to which I am so much indebted in writing this volume, had to sift his copious materials very thoroughly, and to verify with especial care whatever concerned her relation to Goethe, gives in unmistakable language his opinion of how much " Iphigenia" owed to Charlotte. On the second page of his chapter embracing 1779 and 1780, he says : " 'Iphigenia' grew to be a poetic glorification of the calm which Charlotte had at last brought into the soul of the impetuous, susceptible poet. This radiant poem is the first full fruit of the happy change wrought in him through the tranquillizing influence of her affectionate confidence."

X.

SOCIETY.

In these years Charlotte basked in the sunny summer of her long life. The duke esteemed and admired, and was proud of her, as an honor and ornament to his court. On account of her character and judgment she was looked up to by the duchess and beloved as a personal friend. With Herder she was intimate, and had a high weekly enjoyment in his preaching. She found, likewise, a good friend in Knebel, tutor to the duke's younger brother, Prince Constantine, and a distinguished member of the circle of Weimar "aristocrats," the friend and correspondent of Goethe for more than fifty years, a man of culture and social sprightliness; and she was on friendly terms with Seckendorf and Einsidel, both cultivated men of society. In her own family she had recently made an acquisition by the marriage of her brother with Countess Bernsdorf, a captivating little woman whom she took to her heart. Charlotte was enabled to be a comfort to her mother, whose husband, the arbitrary old court-marshal, did not improve with age. She had also much happiness in her remaining children, three boys, the youngest, Fritz, two years old when Goethe came to Weimar, and a pet of the poet, with whom he took up his abode for days and weeks at a time, Goethe making of him, as he grew larger, a companion on short excursions.   Charlotte was not averse to company, showed herself often at court, and frequented the theater.

Weimar being a "residentz," that is, a princely capital, the court was the center and arbiter of social relations.   How much the life and quality of "society" depended upon the spiritual heat and light dispensed by the sovereigns of a small German capital is briefly summed by a line in one of Goethe's letters after a visit to Carlsruhe, the capital of Baden: "Good Heaven! what a paradise Weimar is!" Even though embowering his innocent Eve, Charlotte (who had not within her devil enough to be tempted into disobedience), Weimar, of which himself was the chief figure and beauty, never seemed to him an Eden, until, under the prosaic pressure of the dull court of Carlsruhe, the little Saxon capital sprang up in his memory buoyant and sparkling.   As the exclamation was made in one of his confidential letters to Charlotte, there may have been in it a flavor of irony, appreciable only by her, who knew his intimate thoughts.

But although no other "residentz" shone as Weimar did, Carlsruhe may have been at the period of Goethe's visit exceptionally stupid. Certain it is that the revival of letters in Germany, in the middle of the eighteenth century, touched with its electric wand several of the heads of German principalities. Weimar, as we have seen, was specially favored in having acquired by marriage the Duchess Amalia, beneficently prompted to plant poetry and the higher thought in her capital in the person of Wieland, — a truly imperial performance, and an example which her son, Karl August, had the capacity and the noble impulse to follow, and to better, by clinging to Goethe as his friend and counselor and minister and monitor, thus making Weimar the chief seat in Germany of high mental activity for the culture of letters, science, art, and the beautiful.

In this planting and culture of what advances and elevates humanity, the beautiful plays a decisive part; for, from its sleepless requirements, from its purifying action, thought gets the temper that gives to it a penetrating edge. Under the incitement of the beautiful the worker or thinker, whatever his sphere or province, seeks ever the best that the subject and conditions can furnish. He is impelled onward and upward by an irresistible, restless force, whose life is a subtle stream of light from the infinite creative source; and thus, he who is privileged to act and think by the illumination of this stream, gets to be creative, embodying in his work some of the divine energy whence spring in eternal splendor and power the countless suns of the universe.

This spiritual agency of the beautiful is all-pervasive, brightening with its rays the whole of existence, from the lowly violet to the overhanging canopy of heaven. The legislator as well as the poet, the artisan as well as the artist, in order to have a success, must work under its guidance. In the spring of 1851, in Paris, my boot-maker (Navarre, *Rue de Lille*) brought to me, one Sunday, a pair of boots, and after some talk together about French politics and its leaders, he took from his pocket and read to me a satirical poem on Lamartine, not as a poem so superior as the boots were as boots, but a good poem, well conceived, well executed, both verse and boots wrought under the same aspiring impulse that drove their

makcr to aim at the highest, and that helped
him to reach his aim. Navarre was a poetical
boot-maker. In him the artisan was imbued
with the spirit of the artist.

And with the spirit of the artist all men
must be somewhat imbued who would give life
to their sayings and doings and surroundings,
and especially if they would give to them grace
and captivation. Through social intercourse,
this spirit, a creative spirit, must play as the
sun plays through natural scenery, if this intercourse is to have light and shade, perspective,
variety, a sparkle in places. Without some of
this spirit, "society" is dull, monotonous, unre-
freshing, as Carlsruhe was to Goethe. What
made Weimar seem a paradise in comparison,
was the mental culture which himself was doing so much to promote. For general social
success there is needed tact, sense of proportion, deference, kindliness. Mental culture is
pretty sure to be attended by refinement, although not necessarily by grace of manners.
For good conversation, which is the very life-
blood of good society, culture is indispensable.
Madame de Staël, whose principal object in
coming to Weimar was to talk with Goethe
and Schiller, says of conversation: "The kind
of agreeable feeling caused by an animated

conversation does not exist precisely in the
subject of that conversation : neither the ideas
nor the knowledge therein exhibited make its
principal interest ; that is derived from a
certain manner of acting on one another, of
giving pleasure reciprocally and rapidly, of
speaking the moment one thinks, of an in-
stantaneous enjoyment of one's self, being ap-
plauded without exertion, of manifesting one's
mind in all its shades by accent, gesture, look ;
in short, to produce at will a kind of electricity
which makes sparks fly out, relieves some of
the very excess of their vivacity, and awakens
others from a painful apathy."

Might it not be said that conversation, like
society, is good in proportion as each participant suppresses the egotistic self in him for
the general profit and enlivenment ? Figure to
yourself a dozen people seated round the table,
each one eagerly seeking to utter his individual opinion because it is his, substituting, with
lively affirmation, his subjectivity for the objectivity of eternal principles and of final predominant truth, his subjectivity one-sided and
intolerant in the ratio of his ignorance. This
is not social converse ; it is dissocial, the opposite of what society should be, and must be,
if it would not only attract but endure. The

originating and vivifying principle of social union is, the divesting one's self of personal, local, provincial peculiarities and limitations and littlenesses in order to come together for mental interchange on the high broad ground of universal truth, of disinterested interests. That man is the best talker who — of course without diffuseness or heaviness which kill conversation — can ascend the highest into the region of generic truths, embodying in choice speech the finest verities and possibilities of human feeling and thought. So much the better for him and the company, if at times he can twinkle with wit, which, if genuine, is a joyous sparkle of truth. It was probably on account of his handling with ease such verities and possibilities that the long monologues of Coleridge were borne with by all and admired by many. Having a rich, philosophical mind, fed by widest knowledge and inspired by genius, he dealt in broad principles and eloquent appeals to what is deepest and grandest in human nature, and with such rapt fervor that in his intellectual flight he became lost in the empyrean to his hearers, who could no longer see the drift of his fluent discourse ; nevertheless, like the sky-lark who is heard when so high as not to be visible, there was still audible some of the diviner music of humanity.

XI.

GOETHE was one of those superior natures
that seem to transform themselves on entering
a new field, but who, in fact, only unfold themselves. As Sainte-Beuve says, in a paper on
Cardinal de Retz, "a man is only superior on
this condition, that he have in him that which
transforms and renews, and which is equal to
all great occasions." Goethe had now been
more than four years in Weimar, and had got
so far in informing with a new spirit the administration of the duchy that his beneficent
power began to be felt and acknowledged, and
the early confidence of the duke in him to be
justified. He was fond of refreshing and re-
plenishing his tasked mind with the holiday of
travel. He longed, too, to see his parents. In
the autumn of 1779 he planned a journey with
the duke through Frankfort, up the Rhine into
Switzerland. On the journey he wrote dili-
gently to Charlotte.

The privilege it was of Charlotte, the glorious, the unique privilege, a privilege never enjoyed by any other woman in history, to be for ten years the confidential correspondent of a man so richly endowed, of so great a genius. Charlotte von Stein would have been a distinguished woman, had she never known Goethe ; for she had the high character and the clear intellect and the culture and the refinement that give distinction to man or woman. It was her peculiar, her noble relation to the ardent young poet, to the greatly gifted, aspiring man, that makes her personality and her life so attractive, so valuable to all who value poetic eminence. One of Goethe's reliances, his sweetest resource, was to pour out to her his joys and his troubles, the conceptions and discoveries of his intellect, the movements of his soul. To commune with her through his pen was some indemnification when he could not see his speech reflected in her countenance. Thence he wrote, almost daily, notes when at home in Weimar, within a few minutes' walk of her door.

Just before he started, Goethe announced to his mother their coming, and adds : " I have all that a man can desire, a life in which I daily train myself and daily grow ; and I come this time in health, without passion, without

9

confusion, without hollow pursuit, but like one
beloved of God, who has spent half of his life,
and out of past suffering hopes much good
for the future, and has prepared his breast for
future suffering. If I find you happy I shall
with joy return to the daily work and anxieties
that await me."

From Frankfort, on the twentieth September, he writes to Charlotte: " My old friends
are much rejoiced. The evening of our arrival we were received with beacon-lights. I
found my father changed ; he is more tranquil
and his memory is not so good ; my mother is
still in her old vigor and love. Adieu, best
one ; I expect to-day a note from you. We
shall soon move farther away from you, but
not with hearts. Adieu, greet all." Making
but a short stay at Frankfort, his next letter is
from opposite Speier on the Rhine. Wedel is
the duke's master of the forests, who accompanied them. " On this journey I recapitulate
all my former life, see again all my old acquaintance. It agrees admirably with the duke,
Wedel enjoys himself. Switzerland lies before
us, and we hope by the favor of Heaven to
move about among the grand forms of the
world and to bathe our spirits in the sublime
of nature."

On this journey it was that he described to Charlotte visits he made to Frederika and Lili. Account of these happy meetings with old loves the curious reader will find in Lewes's admirable " Life of Goethe " and in the writer's volume, " Goethe, his Life and Works." From Emindingen, where he visited his sister's grave, he says : " To see Lavater and to have the duke know him better is my greatest hope. I discourse to you only about myself. It is my old sin. Adieu."

From these letters, which are partly in the form of diary, I extract only here and there passages that are biographically or psychologically significant. Having just come from the Bernese glaciers, he writes from Thun on the fourth of October : " Had I been alone I should have gone higher and deeper, but with the duke I must do what is moderate. Still I could allow ourselves more if he had not the bad way to lard pork, and when one has, with pains and danger, reached the summit of the mountain, he will with pains and danger, without object or necessity, seek some other little elevation. By this I have been at times so put out, that last night I dreamed that I had thrown myself with him off from one of them, had left him, and evaded the people he sent after me with all kinds of cunning devices. But when I see that every one has a stake driven into his flesh, which he must drag about with him, and how the duke is really profiting by this journey, all is forgotten. He has an admirable way of observing, of getting interested, of curiosity, shames me often when he insists upon seeing or learning something which I had forgotten or was indifferent to."

A few days later he concludes as follows: "It will be some time yet before we see one another, but when we get through I shall come back to you again. Lavater writes me: 'In the terrible barrenness in living men thou canst think what good it will do me to warm myself at thee?' And I may well say, *children love one another.* Of a truth we don't know what we have in each other, when we have each other all the time. Adieu."

At the beginning of November they were at Geneva. One can understand how a Goethe would not feel at home in the ancient citadel of Calvin, with its provincialism, its musty odor of theology, its traces of Calvinism, traces uncomfortably recognizable in the pharisaical self-satisfaction which pseudo-Christian dogmatism leaves behind it, like foot-prints in mud hardened by frost, which there has not

yet been sun enough to efface. He writes :
" Geneva has thrown me back upon myself ;
for all the world I would not stay a week in
this hole.

" That the French, too, are enchanted with
my *Werther* I should not have conjectured.
To the compliments paid me hereon, I answer
that it is unexpected to me. I am asked
whether I am not going to write another book
of the same sort, and I say : God protect me
from falling into the state in which to write
and to be able to write such another. Meanwhile this echo from the distance gives me
more interest in my things : perhaps in future
I shall be more industrious and shall not waste
as heretofore the good hours. Ade."

. Goethe seems to have been fascinated by
Lavater, to whom he attached himself with all
the closeness of his affectionate nature. How,
with his rare gift of insight into men, he should
have so exaggerated Lavater's qualities, intellectual and moral, as he did in the extract I am
about to make, is inconceivable ; for Lavater
was rather a mystical sentimentalist than a
thinker, a man of lively superficial talent, fitted
for temporary, or even momentary influence,
and no more deserving to be promoted to the
category of great men than Spurgeon or

Beecher is to be put beside Coleridge. And
Goethe who, through personal fascination, so
largely overrated Lavater in the first years of
their acquaintance, underrated him as widely
afterwards, and ceased to correspond with him,
from discovering in him, as he thought, hollowness and dissimulation. These defects may
have shown themselves more prominently as
Lavater grew older, and the more offensively
to Goethe as himself grew more solid with
years, which Lavater did not do. The later de-
preciatory judgment by Goethe seems to have
been as much too strong as the early overesti-
mate of him certainly was. Reaction from one
extreme to the other was probably the greater
from a consciousness in Goethe of early infat-
uation.

The travelers having arrived in Zurich,
where Lavater resided, Goethe writes at the
end of November: "Acquaintance with Lavater is for the duke and me what I hoped it
would be, the seal and highest peak of the
whole journey, and a pasture on the border of
heaven, of which we shall long trace the good
effects. The excellence of this man no mouth
can speak ; when from absence the idea of him
is weakened, his being surprises one anew.
He is the best, greatest, wisest, most cordial

of all the mortal and immortal men whom I
know. Adieu. The post starts, and yesterday
I was lazy."

The reader has had many samples from
Goethe's letters to Charlotte von Stein ; would
he (or she) like to see a letter from him to her
husband, the baron? Here is one that is significant in several ways, dated Zurich, November 30th : " It is very good of you, dear Stein,
to continue giving us accounts of the jovial
condition of our dear Weimar. Don't let time
hang heavy on you until we come back, and
write me again to Frankfort, for which we
start soon. We have been some time in Zurich and have a good life with Lavater, see all
cabinets, drawings, engravings, men and ani-
mals. We lodge in a magnificent public house,
which stands beside the bridge that unites the
town, with a lovely view of the river, lake, and
mountains, etc., have an excellent table, good
beds, and thus all that in enchanted castles is
extemporized for the refreshment of knights.
We have still before us the lake of Constance
and the falls of the Rhine, whither good fortune
will also attend us. Be good enough to have
the inclosed notes delivered, and at Philip's
accompanying request to give to Goezzen a
bunch of keys out of my back or front room.

Adieu. Fare ye well and greet all lovely ladies. G.

" Beg your wife to take an opportunity to
read to the duchess my diary of our journey."

On the way back they got, on the first of
January, 1780, to Darmstadt, south of, and not
far from, Frankfort. They had just visited Stüt-
gardt and Carlsruhe, the capitals of Würtemberg and Baden. How finished a courtier the
poet had grown to be, is shown in a letter to
Charlotte from Darmstadt, in which he complains that since they have become inmates of
courts and move about in the so-called great
world there is no longer life in his letters, and
adds : " It is incredible how intercourse with
people with whom one has little in common
consumes the poor traveler : often I am hardly
conscious that I have been in Switzerland.
Adieu, and happy new year : I must stop, my
pen is too miserable, and in a palace, as you
know, nothing is to be had." Two days later
he continues in the same vein from Homburg,
a very small *residentz*, close to Frankfort :
" Thus we pass from court to court, freeze and
are bored, eat badly and drink even worse.
Here the people move one's pity. They are
unfittingly established, and are mostly sur-

rounded by beggars." This letter he thus concludes: " Soon it will be said of us no longer,
they are coming, but, they are come."

And come they did, after an absence of four
months. They came refreshed and strengthened
in body and mind. In this animated, variegated
journey the duke had gained more than a year's
experience of the world and of himself. The
mentor was rejoiced by the pupil's improvement, and besides this, his chief joy, had himself been gladdened in many ways. He had
embraced again his father and mother, whom
he had not seen for four years ; had enjoyed
the honest pride of bringing with him as fel-
low-guest to lodge under their roof, his sovereign, who was his devoted friend ; and he had
had the very precious privilege of witnessing
their joy and their pride in their now renowned
upmounting son. He had stood face to face
again with Frederika and Lili, and the relief it
was to his conscience to find them both happy
was the main source of his happiness in seeing
them once more. Renewal of personal intercourse with Lavater, especially in company
with Karl August, was a high satisfaction. In
presence of the falls of the Rhine, he and
Lavater had a discussion on the sublime, to the
entertainment and instruction of the duke.

Travel always replenished Goethe's mind with
new images and enlivening experiences, and
before the grandeurs of the Alps he had felt
himself elevated, expanded.

And Charlotte, — what a day when she could
shake warm hands with her dear fellow-trav-
eler ; for Goethe, by his letters and diary, sent
at all opportunities, had made her a participant
of the journey in its every stage. How glad,
too, she was to have Weimar, after its four
months of twilight, re-illuminated by the fer-
vid beams of her genial pupil, and of her pupil's pupil. Charlotte disciplined Goethe and
Goethe disciplined Karl August. What a trio,
with a woman at its summit ! Such a mutuality of improvement is a rare and ennobling
spectacle. What the woman must have been
who could discipline and elevate Goethe ! And
how rich and upstriving a moral nature his was,
to be capable of such refined discipline. We
shall see in the next chapter, even more distinctly than hitherto, what his feelings towards
Charlotte were, and what his acknowledged obligations.

But before closing this chapter it will be well
to report the judgment of Weimar upon the
effect of the journey, a judgment given through
the pen of a very faithful echo of " Society's "

opinion, the sprightly Wieland. A few days after the return of the travelers he writes to Merck : " This Swiss journey, from what I can learn of it from the best sources, belongs among Goethe's masterly dramatic performances. But at the same time one must admit that he is assuredly the *enfant gaté* of nature and all the gods of fate, fortune, and accident ; for, after all, with the whole of his dramatic energy, he would not have been able to blow away a single fatal cloud from the sky, and a single unlucky accident, for which none but a fool would have held him responsible, — but for which the whole world would have held him responsible, — was sufficient to ruin the whole drama."

XII.

In the beginning of October, 1780, the duke
and Goethe paid a visit to Charlotte at Kochberg. The day on which Goèthe returned to
Weimar, he writes to Charlotte a letter which,
as showing the deeper folds of the bond which
held them together, is one of the most interesting in the immense series of notes and letters
writen to her by Goethe : —

"(Tuesday) the tenth of October, evening.
How the states of life stand related to one another like waking and dreaming !

" What you said to me this morning, at the
last moment, pained me very much, and had
not the duke accompanied me up the hill, I
should have had a full fit of weeping. Upon
one evil everything heaps itself up ! It is like
wreaking one's rage against one's own flesh,
when the poor wretch seeks to relieve himself
by insulting her who is dearest to him ; and if
it were only done in a momentary mood, and I
could be conscious of it, but with my thousand

thoughts I am reduced to the condition of a child, ignorant of the moment, in the dark about myself, while the condition of the other person I devour as with a bright, consuming fire.

"I shall not be satisfied until you shall have laid before me a literal account of the past, and for the future strive to endue yourself with so sisterly a feeling that you would not be affected by anything of this kind ; otherwise, I should have to avoid you at those very times when I most need you. It seems to me frightful to be obliged to spoil the best hours of life, those of my being with you, for I would willingly pull out singly every hair of my head, if I could turn it into a kindness; and then to be so blind, so willful. Have compassion on me."

Here we have a glimpse into the tender soul whence was drawn the everlasting life of those beautiful, tragic creations, Mignon and Margaret and so many others. Such impersonations can only spring out of the individual man's rich, warm heart, prompting the ready intellect to their embodiment. No ingenuity, no imitation, no mere art can, without personal sources of sensibility, place before us the living, affecting personages of real poetry.

A few days later he writes : —

"(Friday) the 13th, at night: Through the carrier and Stein I have something from you; now I am tranquil and happy when you say something to me.

"It is extraordinary, and yet it is so, that I am jealous and foolish as a small youngster when you are kindly in your greeting of others. Good-night. For these few days I have not yet recovered my calm, except when asleep."

There is something touching in the contrast between these two letters and his usual cheerful cordiality. In the early summer, on the occasion of Charlotte's absence on a visit to her sister Imhoff in Nuremberg, he had written to her: "A love and confidence without bounds are become a habit with me."

On the seventh of November he has recovered the old tone: "To-day are five years since I came to Weimar. I am very sorry that I cannot celebrate my lustrum with you.

"Yesterday we had beautiful weather, and came very pleasantly hither. [He and the duke from Kochberg.] To be again perfectly sure of your love, makes a great difference to me. With us it should be as with Rhine wine, we must grow better every year. I review my life and come upon extraordinary things. Man is like the night-walker, he reaches the most dangerous precipices while asleep. Keep me in your love; that must strengthen us, so that all that is good shall become closer to us and more lasting; the rest falls away from us daily like shells and scales." And a week later he writes: "As the day breaks I have the wish to be with you again, and accept your invitation to dinner. I hope the Council will be short. Should it be prolonged, sit down to table and put something aside for me." Another short note on the twenty-fourth of November: "I thank you for your sympathy. The inevitable must be borne. Only I beg you to say to yourself daily, that anything in me that could be disagreeable to you, comes from a source over which I have no control. Thereby you will make easier to me much. Adieu. To-day is Council and has been a day of poetic rest."

It is not easy to fathom the depth of the service to Goethe of the affection between him and Charlotte von Stein. She drew to herself the passionate susceptibility toward woman of this warm-souled man, and kept it alive and pure, and alive because pure, during ten years of his young manhood. She tuned his whole being to a higher key. The hourly thought of her was a perpetual perfume that sweetened all his multifarious work. The days and years

now flowed on for her happily in the wonted
current of domestic and social duties, for him
in the zealous performance of the highest human tasks, his activity as poet, as statesman,
as man, encouraged by her admiration, cheered
by her affection, soothed by her sympathy and
sisterly, and more than sisterly, devotion, her
whole bearing ennobled, and made more attractive by the self-control of the chaste wife,
the conscientious mother.

Is there in biography a record of any other
very eminent man being similarly influenced
by a woman? The friendship and reciprocal
admiration between Michelangelo and Vittoria
Colonna presents a likeness if not a parallel;
for Michelangelo was sixty when he first met
with Vittoria, and she forty-five. Her acquaintance and sympathy were a great though late
comfort to the noble, wronged, proud, rugged
giant. They were attracted to each other by
corresponding high qualities and gifts. Her
gentle influence warmed the tenderness there
lay in the great heart of the mighty artist, and
the pictures he painted for her are said to have
been more inspired by love than most of his
other work. On receiving one she had ordered,
which he had finished with great care, she sent
him a letter which, after warmly praising his

work and telling him that he "adds excellence to things already perfect," she concludes: "I must tell you that I rejoice that the angel on the right hand is so beautiful, for the Archangel Michel will place you, Michelangelo, on the right of the Lord on that day. Meanwhile I do not know how to serve you better, than to pray for you to this sweet Christ, whom you have so well, so perfectly, painted, and to beseech you that you may command me as altogether yours in all things."

The friend of Michelangelo, and his pupil as well as biographer, Ascanio Condivi, distinctly describes in a few lines the relation between him and Vittoria: "He greatly loved Vittoria, the marchioness of Pescara, of whose divine spirit he was enamored, while for him in return her love was as devoted, expressed to him in many sweet and pure letters which he possesses, whilst he wrote to her many sonnets full of fancy and gentle friendship. She frequently went to Viterbo and other places to spend the summer, coming at times to Rome for no other reason but to see Michelangelo; and he on his part so loved her that I remember hearing him say that when he went to see her on her death-bed, he lamented he had not kissed her face as he did her hand."

In the "Banquet" Plato attributes to Socrates a discourse on Love, — Love in the most comprehensive sense, the high thoughts of which, Socrates says, he had from Diotima, called the prophetess of Mantenea. By this means Plato probably meant to make known the opinions of Socrates, as he, Plato, had often heard them from him, as to the power of intuition in women. Socrates was not entirely in advance of his country and age in regard to women, to whom, by the Greeks, in their partial development, was then allotted an inferior place; but from this account of Diotima, to whom, he is made by Plato to say, he was under great mental obligations, from his friendship and admiration for Aspasia, and from the high opinion he had of his own mother, he evidently had a clearer, truer perception of the capacity and power of women. From the profound and beautiful symmetry there is in the human organization, men of large, susceptive, creative minds, like Socrates and Goethe, are very apt to entertain like views on deep psychical questions. In "Wilhelm Meister" Goethe has embodied in Macaria a woman who, like the Diotima of Socrates, has on the most momentous soul-questions a sure, searching judgment, a judgment drawn from the intuitional power possessed in the highest degree only by woman when she happens to be exceptionally gifted, — a power largely shared by the highest masculine minds, when they enjoy the privilege of being endowed with the feminine principle, "the eternal womanly," as Goethe calls it.

"We enter on one of the most beautiful years of the poet:" with these words Schoell opens 1781. The cloud, which in the preceding autumn had cast a sudden shadow over him, had not only passed away, but the sunshine that followed seems to have been warmer and more cheerful than any he yet owed to his intimacy with Charlotte. Besides showering upon her, in his daily notes, expressions of endearment, of thankfulness, of benediction, which only a prolific poet, sincere as well as imaginative, could thus multiply, he calls her "the light of all his days." Her mind "helps him create;" her affection "makes for him a delightful climate." In the fullness of his trust, in the stimulation of his genius by the joy he took in communing with her, he gives voice, too, to deepest words of wisdom, to noblest truths: "On this shifting ball of earth there is only joy and peace in genuine love, in doing good, and in ever learning." "I pray God to make me every day more economical, that I may be able to be generous." "Thy approval is my best fame, and if I value a good name in the world, it is on thy account, that I may be no disgrace to thee." Having her youngest boy, Fritz, with him on a journey, he says : " Christ was right to refer us to children ; from them we can learn how to live and to become blessed."

In March, Goethe and the duke paid a visit to Neunheiligen, the castle of Count and Countess Werther. From a long letter to Charlotte, on the eleventh, I translate two or three passages : "The countess has given me many a new thought, and brought the old ones closer together. You know I never learn anything except through irradiation, that only nature and the greatest masters can make anything intelligible to me, and that to seize a thing by halves or isolated is to me utterly impossible." " I see and hear nothing good that I do not instantly share with you ; and all my observations on the world and myself are addressed, not like Mark Antony's, to my own, but to my second self." Here is a picture of Countess Werther which has a twofold charm, as a sketch of a high-bred lady of remarkable tact, and as an example of Goethe's fine perception : " This little being has enlightened

me: she has such knowledge of the world and
she knows how to deal with the world; she is
like quicksilver, which in a moment divides
itself into a thousand parts and runs again
into a ball. Sure of her worth and her rank,
she bears herself with a delicacy and ease,
which one must see in order to understand it.
She seems to give each one his own, when she
gives nothing: she does not deliver, as I have
seen others do, to each according to his rank
and position, the sealed destined little packet;
she carries herself with a seemingly thought-
less impartiality; and precisely thence comes
the beautiful melody which she produces, because she does not dwell on each tone but
only on the choicest, touching it with a light-
ness and such seeming carelessness, that one
might take her for a child who, without looking
at the notes, runs over the keys of a piano,
but she always knows what and to whom she
plays. What in each art is genius she has in
the art of life. A thousand others seem to me
like people who through industry would make
up for what nature has denied them; others,
like amateurs, who learn their little concert by
rote and produce it painfully; others — but it
will give us material for conversation. She
knows the greatest part of distinguished, afflu-

ent, beautiful, intelligent Europe, partly through
herself, partly through others ; the life, doing,
relations of very many people is present to her
in the highest sense of the word. What she
appropriates to herself from each becomes
her, and what she gives to each does him
good. You see I step quickly on all sides, in
order, by means of dead words and a series of
expressions, to describe a single living picture.
The best remains ever behind. I have still
three days, and nothing to do but to observe
her ; in that time I shall yet master many a
trait. Only one more, which like a parabola
indicates the beginning of an immense range.
The parson here is a bad fellow, not so that he
could be deposed, but bad. When the count invites him to dinner she comes not to the table,
and says it is right and necessary to show
openly when you despise any one on account
of his badness. Put this with the foregoing and
the sum total is multiplied enormously."

From another long letter, written the following day, here are two short passages : " Our
poor, lovely hostess is ill, and bears it as women
are wont to do. This morning we had a long
political conversation ; and these things she
sees beautifully and naturally like her sex."
" The Jews have cords which they wind about

the arm when they pray ; so do I wind round my arm thy dear band when I pray that I may partake of thy goodness, wisdom, moderation, and patience. I beg thee, on my knees, complete thy work, make me right good." After his return to Weimar he says in a note of the twenty-fifth March : "On 'Tasso' nothing will be done to-day. But do you not observe how love provides for your poet. Months ago the next scene was impossible to me : how easily it now flows out of my heart. My love, for these five years past, comes filing before me with so beautiful a line of many good sentiments. Oh, could I say to thee, what I owe to thee !" At the end of a note on the twenty-second of April he calls her : " Thou, the fulfillment of my many thousand wishes."

These last words almost suffice to justify a rumor, mentioned in letters of contemporaries, but not alluded to, probably from delicacy, by either Schoell or Duentzer, that Goethe wished Charlotte to be divorced from Baron von Stein in order that she might be united in marriage with him. In Germany, at that time, divorces, with a direct view to other unions, were not uncommon, as was seen in the case of the Imhoffs. Where husband and wife concurred, and jointly applied, divorce was readily granted.

That the marriage of Stein and Charlotte was not annulled was said to be owing to the opposition of her family. In the absence of positive proof that there was such a project, we have to look to circumstantial evidence, and that chiefly drawn from the letters of Goethe to Charlotte in the years 1781-2-3-4-5. In these, compared with those of the preceding five years, there is a deepening of feeling, a heightening of tone, a significant emphasis. He resumes, almost permanently, the affectionate *du*, and in one of his notes complains of her not reciprocating this tender form of address. The letters and notes are warmer and more frequent. He seems not to be able to get through a day without telling her with his pen of his love and devotion, and telling this with such variety and richness of endearing expressions and epithets as only the inspired ingenuity of an impassioned lover and imaginative poet could have extemporized. Could admiration, confidence, devotion, and gratitude be more freshly and cordially and impressively uttered than in the following note of the 27th March, 1781? "The openness and calm of my heart, which thou hast restored to me, be also for thee alone, and all the good for others and myself that shall thence arise be likewise thine.

Believe me, I feel myself changed; my old well-doing has returned, and with it the joy of my life. Thou hast given me the joy of doing good which I had lost. Adieu. Thus may I ever continue: and be it in presence or on paper, how hard it is for me to part from thee."

From Ilmenau, July 8th, he writes this post-script, which points more distinctly than anything yet quoted to the rumor above alluded to: "In anxious moments thy foot and thy children's cough torment me. We are truly married, that is, bound by a band, the woof of which consists of love and joy, and the web of cross, trouble, and misery. Adieu: greet Stein. Help me to believe and to hope."

The same tone runs through all the notes and letters of these years. It is difficult not to make from them many more extracts, they so glisten with the light of chastened affection and are so glowing with beauty and wisdom. In April, 1782, he writes from the neighborhood of Eisenach: "I feared thou might'st be ill, and thy letter gives me the sad certainty. Hope, which ever kindly deceives us, tells me that thou art already better again. Is it not true, dearest, that thou know'st I never swerve from thee. Would that I were with thee, that I

might wait upon and tend thee." Again, two
days later : " Thy last note caused in me many
sorrowful thoughts ; in the night I wept bit-
terly, as I imagined that I might lose thee.
Against everything that is likely to happen to
me I have a counterweight in myself, against
this, nothing.   Hope helps us to live.   Now I
think again thou art well and wilt be well when
thou receiv'st this note."   Again, in the same
letter : " What do I not owe to thee, dearest ?
Even if thou didst not so distinguish me with
thy love, if thou only bore with me along with
others, I should still be bound to dedicate my
whole being to thee.   For, should I have been
able without thee to renounce my pet errors ?
Or could I see the world so clearly, conduct
myself in it so successfully, as since I have
nothing more to seek in it ? "   Here, on the
occasion of some one's being deserted by pat-
rons, is a piece of wisdom which holds good
for all times and places : " But woe to him who
allows himself to be tempted by the favor of
the great into the open field, without having
first protected his rear."   Here is another sentence still deeper, and which could only come
from one in whom the intellect was clear and
piercing, the heart warm and deep : " Oh, dear
Lotte, how badly off are most people ! how

narrow is their life-circle and whither does it run! We two, on the contrary, have treasures wherewith we could out-buy kings : let us in quiet enjoy what we are blessed with."

Before closing this long chapter I must make one more extract. Goethe, at the end of the year 1782, was passing a week in Leipzig, and thus concludes his last letter : "With the general treatment of me, I am very well satisfied. They show me the best will and the greatest respect ; on my part, I am friendly, attentive, communicative, and civil to every one. It is very gratifying to be a stranger in a place, and yet so necessary as to find there a home. Oh, dear Lotte, I owe to thee my happiness at home, and my enjoyment abroad ; for the calmness, the equanimity, with which I receive and give, rests on the ground of thy love. Farewell. To-day I hope for a letter from thee, with news that thou art well. Adieu, my dear one, my only one ! My life, my charm.

"Greet the duke and say to him that I leave this on Thursday, but shall probably not arrive before Friday, because we others cannot make such a journey in a day.

"Greet Stein and the children and the little one."

XIII.

FROM a few samples of Goethe's acknowledgments to Charlotte we have seen what she was to him, what a blessing to his life. In absence the thought of her was a delightful companionship. To his mind she was ever present, an encouragement, a tranquillization, a guardian spirit. The hours spent with her were his dearest, his most precious.

To Charlotte the love of Goethe was an elevating prerogative; it was an ever-renewed invigoration to her being. Through the daily round of cares and duties, of doubts and fulfillments, of petty hopes, and petty disappointments, their mutual affection ran like a vivid artery that brought freshening currents and color to the dullest routine. She lived a double life, a life of reality, like her neighbors, and a life, not less real, of enchantment, wrought and furnished by the magic power of a great poet, of a man genial, sociable, brilliant, this second life interfusing the other with golden beams of empyreal illumination, besparkling it with ever-returning rainbows, overhanging it with worshipful transfiguration.

Her friendliness and intelligence and culture and manners drew around Charlotte a circle of friends whom her sincerity held attached to her. To one of these, the wife (*née* Countess Bernsdorf) of her youngest brother, she writes in June, 1784, from Kochberg: "Here everything is dry and empty, and the spirit of God hovers over the dryness. My chief pastime is to sit near the door on the bridge, and there I have a right to sing : —

> 'O'ershadowed by the poplar-tree,
> Beside the moss-green brook.'

I long for no guests but thee. Greet my brother and the Herders. Farewell, thou good one, and keep me in thy love." Two weeks later she writes to the same : " Only imagine, that as yet I have not played once on the piano, have drawn hardly four times. I have so much to write, that whole days are given to it ; and to the household I give attention, too ; for I am studying 'The Housemother,' and go sometimes into the cow-stable and get an excellent insight into how I am cheated, without being able to help myself."

About this time Charlotte felt herself called upon at Kochberg to look into the conduct of those affairs upon which depended the income of the estate; for the baron, by experiments made without shrewdness, and expenditures without knowledge, was getting his finances into a worse, instead of a better state through his economic activity, verifying one of Goethe's many wise sayings, that " nothing is so frightful as active ignorance." Stein was very liable to be cheated, a liability which is ever quickly discerned by those who, like his steward, are in a position to make dishonest profit out of it. The baron prided himself on his good-nature; but, in certain relations, what to him seemed a virtue was the equivalent of foolishness, and a mischievous foolishness.

A life-long friend and appreciator of Charlotte was the high-toned, clear-headed Duchess Louise. From Eisenach, where the court then was, Louise, who seems to have enjoyed the company of courtiers as little as Goethe did, writes to her: "As it seems that husbandry has taken possession of all the faculties of your body and soul to that degree that you cannot think of your female friends (I do not say of your friend), I therefore am moved to begin the correspondence and to impart to you that I am *ennuyée* and am sick. Yesterday, to the great vexation of the whole public, I had to leave the theater from a very necessary cause, and to-day I keep my room, in order to restore my health, which has been ruined by repeated colds. These ever-recurring cramps and mis-chances bode me no good. In spite of what you say for my comfort, I fear and believe that I shall prove to be right. This constant appre-hension is not pleasant. You have no concep-tion how I weary of this kind of men and women, but as little have you of how beautiful and romantic this region is, and how strongly it is in contrast with its inhabitants. Are you alone with your oxen and cows, or have you other company? However this may be, think sometimes of me and don't forget me entirely."

In midsummer, 1786, several friends from Weimar met at Carlsbad, Goethe, Charlotte, the duke, Fräulein Waldner, the Herders. It looked as if they were there to take leave of Goethe; not one of them, however, save the duke, knew that they were about to part with him for many months. Goethe had a belief that to make known a project tends to frus-trate its execution. Thus his purpose of a winter journey to the Hartz Mountains was not even imparted to the duke, and when Karl

August and he went on the Swiss tour, none in Weimar knew whither they were going nor for how long they were to be absent. A similar secrecy he observed in his literary plans: except to Charlotte, in some cases, he spoke to no one of what he was writing or going to write.

Goethe was a man of infinite inward resources and desires; but these, for their full evolution and activity, required fresh food from without, new horizons and opportunities. Early in the summer he wrote to the duke: "Through use of the bath for two years my health is much improved, and I hope also the best for the elasticity of my mind if, left for a while to itself, it can freely enjoy the world." He felt that his mind was beginning to suffer from the constant wear of prosaic public business in the monotonous routine of a contracted circle. He needed refreshment, change, enlargement.

Was there foundation for the rumor about a divorce? Was there a disappointment, and had it any influence on the time of his starting for Italy? These questions cannot be answered confidently. We have only inference from the substance and tone of his letters to Charlotte during the past five years; and even here the inference is somewhat discouraged by the continuance of this tone after he had reached Italy. On the other hand, that he should not have even given a hint to Charlotte of his journey looks as though he had, for breaking away, deep personal reasons that he could not utter to her. Their relation to each other for ten years was unexampled. Goethe, being what he was, it is marvelous that it lasted so long ; that it did last proves the power of Charlotte's elevated attractiveness, and Goethe's elevated capacity to be so firmly held by a chain of purely spiritual mould untempered by corporeal alloy.

Yet it was to cease, this relation ; it was exceptional, it was incomplete. Charlotte could not legitimately have expected that it would last so long. She seems to have been designed, — what a proud, high office, — to strengthen, by refining, Goethe's rich nature in that teeming decade of his exuberant young manhood. It was not a lover's exaggeration, it was not poetical hyperbole, when he called her his guardian-angel. And now his destiny bore him away from her, — his destiny, that is, the momentum made up by his inward impulsions and the urgent solicitations from outward fields of endeavor and improvement. Italy beckoned to him irresistibly. The prints which his father

had brought from that pictorial paradise, and
had hung on his walls, had made on Goethe's
opening susceptive faculties a clean impression,
which his after studies and his inborn procliv-
ities had deepened. Italy, with her beauties
and grandeurs and treasures of nature and art,
was to be his instructress, or his education
would be truncated. And thus his ardent,
pure, and refining relation to Charlotte was to
end. That important part of his education was
finished. It was to end, so far as any mental
influence may be said to end. From high,
moral springs there is such ceaseless onflow of
power that its current can hardly be said to
stop. Indeed, strictly speaking, nothing ends;
there is an everlasting on-going; there is always a future; in some shape or other, there
is always retrieval. Hence what seems con-
summating misfortune, final loss, is often entrance to a new path of improvement. There
are always latent rainbows in the atmosphere:
smiles lie in wait behind tears.

In order to have no hindrance to his freedom from his renown, Goethe entered Italy
under an assumed name. Having left Carlsbad
on the third of September, he was at Verona
on the eighteenth, and wrote thence to Charlotte. By some miscarriage this letter was long

in reaching her. She became anxious and then
fell into deep grief. Believing that he had left
Weimar never to return, his desertion seemed
a breach of faith towards herself. Her distress
uttered itself in two pieces of verse, found
among her papers, which with feeling and sim-
plicity give voice to her pain and loneliness.
The first stanza of one of the short poems I
translate as a sample : —

> " Fly, ye thoughts, that were my own,
> As my friend from me hath flown !
> Of the hours, ye now remind me,
> Spent with him so oft, so kindly.
> Now am I for aye alone,
> Lonely now, for he is gone."

Her trouble was soon relieved, and on
Christmas Day she wrote to her young friend,
Charlotte von Lengefeld (the future wife of
Schiller) in this cheerful mood : " From Goethe
in Rome I have many beautiful letters which I
will let you read when you come to us. That
he will come back to us is certainly his intention, but Heaven often determines otherwise
than we conditioned mortals will. He quitted
his friends a little uncivilly."

On the twenty-seventh of October Goethe
wrote to her from Terni as follows. The last
sentence smacks of the divorce rumor. Had
he yet hopes of that project ? — if there ever

was such a project : " Sitting in a cave which
a year ago suffered from an earthquake, I address my prayer to thee, my dear guardian-
angel ! How spoilt I am, I feel now for the
first time. To live ten years with thee, beloved by thee, and now in a strange world! I
said to myself it would be so, and nothing but
the highest · necessity had power to force me
to take the resolution. Let us have no other
thought than to pass our lives together."

While in Italy Goethe sent her every week
his diary, out of which was afterwards made
up his volume, "The Italian Journey." To his
pet, Fritz, Charlotte's youngest boy, now twelve
years of age, he wrote, on the tenth of March
from Naples, the following letter. His promise to take Fritz to Italy at some future day,
might it not be interpreted as giving color, too,
to the divorce rumor ? " I shall come back so
soon as is possible, so soon as I shall have obtained a certain kind of knowledge of this
country, so soon as I shall have seen what is
most remarkable in nature and art. Then I
will relate much to thee ; we will apply various
considerations, and one of these days I will
bring thyself hither. Make to thyself no
gloomy representations of my remaining away.
It was very needful to me to make my own a

large mass of fresh knowledge, of new ideas, which for a while I can work up. This will be to the advantage of myself and all my friends. Greet Ernest and tell him to write to me what he is about. Commend me to thy grandmother's kind remembrance. I joy in the thought of home from more than *one* cause, and thou art one of the first."

That there had been, during the past year or two, something which caused a difficulty, if not a discord, between Charlotte and Goethe is manifest from a letter dated April the eighteenth, at Palermo. Be the reader assured that could the author find any clew to what this difficulty was he would with alacrity make him or her a sharer in the discovery. But neither Duentzer nor Schoell mention it, except that Schoell refers back to a note penned in Weimar, June the twenty-fifth, 1786, which alludes to something adverse, but which leaves us as much in the dark as to what it was or whence, as the letter from Sicily. Here is the note from Weimar, a very characteristic one : " Do, my dear, what and how shall seem right to thee, and so shall it be to me. Only keep me in your love, and let us at any rate preserve a good, that we shall never find again, even though there be moments when we cannot

enjoy it. I am revising *Werther*, and think
that the author did wrong not to blow out his
brains when he had finished it. To-day Wieland dines with me ; we are sitting in judgment upon ' Iphigenia.' " And this is the con-
clusion of the letter from Palermo': " What I
am preparing for you goes on successfully. I
have already shed tears of joy that I shall give
you pleasure. Farewell, most beloved ! My
heart is with thee, and now that wide distance
and absence have, as it were, cleared away
what lately disturbed us, the beautiful flame of
love, fidelity, and memory burns again and
lights up with joy my heart. Greet the Herders and all and think of me."

To Charlotte these were years of deprivation.
Her second son, Ernest, was ill when Goethe
" quitted his friends so uncivilly," and the following summer he died on the way to Carlsbad.
Some days later she writes to her sister and
little sister-in-law from Carlsbad : " You can
readily understand how empty and uninterest-
ing everything is to me. On the sixteenth of
July I hope to get away from here. I shall be
glad to get home, although I fear some other
trouble is hanging over me. A dream which I
had more than seventeen years ago, I had
again in Wildenthal, where Ernest died. But

nothing more of this ! Life is all a dream, and
you two are to me a most agreeable dream."
On the twenty-third of July she was again in
Weimar, where her sister-in-law brought to her
the unhappy Charlotte von Kalb, "a being,"
says Duentzer, "consumed by an inward lurid
fire," who was then entertaining the thought of
separating from her husband to unite herself to
Schiller, who at Manheim had made a deep
impression upon her. Schiller arrived in Weimar on the twenty-first, and a few days later
Charlotte met him for the first time. On the
twelfth of August Schiller writes to his friend
Koerner (father of the patriot-poet) that he had
been taking a tiresome walk in a company of
nobles, shallow people, " the best among whom
was Frau von Stein, a truly interesting person,
and of whom I can understand that Goethe became so devoted to her. Beautiful she never
can have been, but her countenance has a soft
earnestness, and a quite peculiar openness. A
sound understanding, feeling, and truth lie in
her being. This lady possesses over a thousand letters from Goethe, and from Italy he
writes to her every week. It is said that their
intercourse is perfectly pure and· blameless."
We see, adds Duentzer, that Goethe's strongest
enemies did not dare to say anything against
this relation.

On the first of September Charlotte wrote from Kochberg to her little sister-in-law : " I thank thee, treasure, for thy charming note. My existence here is not entirely poetical as thou describ'st it to me, but that is certain that each year, like as one is to the other, becomes here different. I am happier now, because I am reconciled to the separation from my friend which last year was so bitter to me. Yesterday I was in Kuhfrass and saw the fishing ; we sat in a pleasant little spot on the pond shaded with trees, and lo ! there came the good creatures from Rudolstadt, the Lengefelds, the Beulwitzes, and the little maiden (Frederike von Holleben) who for longing for her lover grows ever thinner. Then we came over here again to Kochberg and drank tea in the poplar shed on the bridge ; then we parted again. The husband was with them, I mean Beulwitz. That is the only thing that untunes me in this angel family. He has cross moods, which amount to rudeness ; his wife turns them off, but they hurt his mother-in-law. Lottchen (Lengefeld) is always with me ; she will write to thee. You have in Weimar celebrated very pleasantly the birthday of the absent (Goethe). I am glad I was not there : I could not be joyful on that day. Herewith I send you the

"Diary of a Ghostseer." It is very good. Give it to Mad. Herder in my name, and greet both for me. Say also a sisterly greeting to thy husband. Give many thanks to Knebel for his note. It is ever my fate to remain in his debt. At an early day I will see if by compressing something out of this barren wilderness in my imagination I can make it seem richer to him. Kiss the hand of the Duchess Louise from me. Goethe will remain in Rome till Easter. Last night I had a singular dream about him : I feared some misfortune was to happen to him at the time he thought of coming back to us."

In the following note, to the same correspondent, Charlotte speaks frankly of her good friend, the duke. Karl August had a soul for a wider sphere of action than a dukedom of two hundred thousand inhabitants could supply ; and he had, moreover, a military ambition, for gratifying which there being no field in his limited dominion, he had entered the Prussian service : "I am very glad that I am not just now in Weimar, and that I declined the compliment the duke paid me of wishing to see me before his departure (for the Prussian army in Holland). When one regards him as an individual, one cannot but love him, and pity him the more because he fails to perceive his true destination. But he feels it not, and men must be what their inward movement makes them. 'If a man's interior is made up of erring substance, who can reason it out of him,' says a wise Hindoo."

While in Italy Goethe finished "Egmont," and sent the manuscript to his friends in Weimar. Charlotte was disappointed ; especially was Claerchen unacceptable to her. She had a woman's shrewd suspicion that the author had found in Rome the model for this, one of his warmest creations. An anxious trial it was for an affectionate, high-spirited woman of forty-five, when a fictitious, but most real, Claerchen came suddenly before her out of Rome, to turn her thoughts still more vividly upon a lover of thirty-eight, absent among "strange women" of a captivating, luxurious type, and that lover of a temperament the opposite of her own, Goethe being of an "amorous complexion."

There was one "friend" of Charlotte of whom little has been said, but who is one of the main supports of our narrative edifice, without whom, indeed, there would have been no Charlotte von Stein. The Baron von Stein was quite competent to his official position in the ducal household, was liked in "society" as a "good fellow," and from what we can now judge, seems to

have been a good husband, as husbands go;
but he was not an aristocrat, and, as our little
book is chiefly about aristocrats, he does not
often appear in its pages, and would not appear
at all had he not happened to give his name to
our heroine, the principal female aristocrat of
the circle. The aristocracy and the common-
alty intermingle but superficially. It has been
seen how the aristocrat, Schiller, on taking a
walk with a company of " nobles," quickly discerned, with the fine instinct of his class, that
they were not of the real but only of the nomi-
nal nobility, and at once singled out Charlotte
as a fellow-aristocrat. Contrive as you will,
decree as you will, begild with titles, overload
with privileges and possessions, there is among
men but one genuine superiority, the superiority of mind, a superiority resulting from the
union of the higher intellect with the higher
feelings. Weimar is to-day a consecrated name
in the thought of the cultivated, because there,
at the end of the last century, was manifested
more conspicuously than elsewhere this mental
superiority. Charlotte von Stein has had in
Germany monumental volumes dedicated to
her, because she was the beloved, pure friend,
the 'confessor, counselor, soother' of him who
asserted this superiority the most solidly and
brilliantly.

It has been seen, from a letter of Goethe's to
Stein, how friendly, one might say, fraternal,
their relations were. Charlotte writes, at the
close of 1787, to Lottchen: " To-day my husband returned from Gotha, and has brought me
beautiful things for Christmas presents, and
is so complaisant towards me that I could wish
to all good wives a like conduct on the part of
their husbands." Was this a flash of conjugal
kindness, gleaming so unexpectedly that she is
surprised into recording it ? Can any light be
derived from it to illuminate the obscurity of
the divorce question ?

If Charlotte had no ground for personal complaint against her own partner, she had cause
to be deeply grieved for her sister Imhoff, whose
husband had grown callous to all sense of
manly duty and propriety, and even decency.
Imhoff had become so impoverished that, when
he came to live in Weimar, he received, through
the influence of his wife's family, a small pension from the duke. No doubt he had in the
beginning exaggerated the amount paid him by
Warren Hastings for giving up to Hastings his
first wife ; and whatever the sum was, having
much more talent for spending than for saving, and being a man of loose structure and
weak judgment, he had found himself, after a

few years, once more straitened. To the passage relating to her own husband Charlotte
adds the following : " My poor sister, Imhoff, is,
on the other hand, most unhappy. It would
distress you, were I to relate to you how badly
her husband now behaves to her, and how he
seeks to dishonor her before the world and
leaves her helpless. My heart often bleeds for
her, and it grieves me that my poor mother
should see one of her children so unhappy.
Ah! if one could only know how it will all end,
how would one fear to begin!"

Lottchen Lengefeld, Charlotte's correspondent, had had, not long before, a wooer, to whom
she was not indifferent, an English captain,
who, however, had to quit Weimar suddenly,
being ordered to India. Her mother would
have liked her to accept the son of the chief
minister of the Principality of Rudolstadt,
where the Lengefelds resided, but to him Lottchen had an aversion. Charlotte was the confidant of her heart, and to her she wrote in
December, that she had in Rudolstadt received
a visit from Schiller, who had said he hoped
soon to see her (Charlotte) in Weimar. To
this Charlotte answers : " Schiller I have only
seen once. I believe he does not care to see
many real people, in order not to be put on a

wrong track with his imagined beings, who are
probably more acceptable to him."

Thus were the Fates spinning the threads
which were to bind Charlotte von Stein to the
second great poet of Germany, — not so closely
as she had been bound to the first ; yet, in an
intimacy that was to be a comfort to her in
times of trouble.   No dream had she then that
her dear Lottchen was to be the wife of Schiller.

XIV.

THE RUPTURE.

In the opening of 1788, Charlotte, in answer to a note from Lottchen, wrote : " Drive away all sad clouds from your soul! One can become master over all evils except want and disease : you suffer from neither, and have, moreover, a dear sister with you. Cheer up, too, your mother. If I could only be always with you. With us everybody is going to Italy ; I say everybody, but this is not quite true : myself, I am for home, and whoever is not well at home, to him it will not be well anywhere, and such a journey is only a palliative. It is different with youth that believes there is something to be got abroad. My poor sister is like a shadow out of the grave ; her bloom and her spirits are all gone. It is not yet decided whether the separation will take place. God grant that it may!"

Duentzer emphatically insists that the above denunciation of travel cannot possibly be aimed at Goethe. It seems to me that it is so

aimed, — a general remark with this particular
application, the generalization itself deduced
from this one individual case, and, like all de-
ductions from single cases, unsound, in this
instance the more unsound, from the curious
unsoundness of the one premise, Goethe having been not well at home and having benefited immeasurably by leaving home for travel
and sojourn abroad. He had broken up his
mode of life in Weimar, which in its action
upon himself, and somewhat even upon others,
had exhausted its usefulness, and which, to his
large, aspiring nature, was growing into an
arid routine, and he had opened in Italy fresh
spheres of knowledge and expectation, which
gave new strength and expansion to his ever
hungering mind. His relation to Charlotte,
improving, elevating, delightful with a peculiar and pure delight, had run its serviceable
course, and he, by a supreme act of will, possible only to strong natures, had shaken off its
sweet dominion and emancipated himself from
its fascination.

This emancipation it was that went so hard
with Charlotte. Power clings to the hands that
wield it, and power wielded by a woman over a
man, especially over a superior man, is the more
tenacious from the very nature of feminine fas-

cination, whose silent subtlety so fastens itself
with willful cohesion in the heart of the wielder,
that when he upon whom it acts rebels, the
wrench of the break is apt to be more agoniz-
ing to her than to him. Goethe's willing, cheerful, absolute subjection to her, while it had
wrought upon her affections had strengthened
her natural pride, and thus had made his falling off a twofold trial; for, that he had fallen
off from his allegiance to her she had an in-
stinctive consciousness, notwithstanding the
continued assurance of devotion in his letters
from Italy. From the first shock of his supposed desertion she had never entirely recovered. And so this, to her unannounced, unexpected, Italian journey was a sore thing to
Charlotte. It had made a sudden cessation to
the happiest, brighest phasis of her life; it dispelled the enchantment which for ten years had
glorified her daily being. Should we not look
indulgently on a high-spirited, sensitive woman
who measured this journey by its consequences
to herself and not by the intellectual æsthetic
good it was doing to Goethe?

In the mean time Weimar started on the
new year with as much spirit and promise as
could be expected in the absence of its chief
motor. About this time the Weimar circle was

enlivened by the arrival, for permanent abode,
of an English family, Charles Gore and his
two daughters Eliza and Emily, acquaintance
with whom the duke and Goethe had made at
Carlsbad, — all three refined, intelligent, cultivated people of high character, in short, genuine aristocrats. The duchess was much attracted to the two well-bred ladies.

Knebel, the translator of " Lucretius," was important enough literarily to have three volumes
of literary remains published, embracing poems,
essays, and letters, many of them from Karl
August, the whole embellished with a portrait
which indicates a man of refinement, intellect,
and excitability.   The life-long friend and correspondent of Goethe, he was also a valued
friend of Charlotte. - He lived at present in
Goethe's garden-house, which Charlotte, to
whom Goethe had given the disposal of it, had
let him have.   In a letter to his sister, Khebel
writes that from Charlotte more than from any
one else he draws nourishment for his life, and
gives the following sketch of her : " Pure right
feeling, and a natural, passionless, easy disposition, with her own industry and association
with superior people, which her appetite for
knowledge made profitable, have formed her
into one, whose being and kind will hardly be

found again in Germany. She is without any
pretension or affectation, upright, simple, free,
neither too heavy nor too light; without enthusiasm and yet with warmth of mind; takes an
interest in all that is rational, and all that is
human; is well-informed, and has fine tact, even
talent for art. She is now drawing heads in
miniature after nature with such fineness, that
Imhoff is only a bungler in comparison. You
can readily believe that, with such qualities,
many are devoted to her."

At last his coming is announced, — the coming of him whose long absence had left a void
which nothing and nobody could supply. The
return of the "distinguished Roman," as Herder called him, Duentzer announces with German circumstantiality: "Goethe arrived on the
eighteenth of July towards ten o'clock in the
evening, with a full moon." Weimar awoke
the next morning with a sense of restoration.
In the mental atmosphere there was a sunshine
there had not been for two years. Goethe
might be almost called the creator of the Weimar of 1788. He was come back, but he was
not the Goethe who had gone away. Goethe
was a great grower, and in Italy he had grown
with unwonted rapidity. In after years he
spoke of this visit to Italy as his re-birth. Here

he had obtained "glimpses into the nature of things and their relations which open to me an abyss of wealth."

His Weimar friends hardly knew what to make of him; he had been moving forward, they had been standing still. They did not understand the new, enlarged Goethe, and he was offended by their unsusceptibility. They showed no sympathy with the enthusiasm for Italy he had brought back with him nor with the expansion of his views, and he was repelled by their apathy. To Charlotte he seemed only changed, not improved, and her indifference chilled him and made her, too, seem changed to him. Both complained of coldness in the other. The dear old bond between them was broken. He had brought back with him, not only new ideas, new knowledge, but new eyes; and, in spite of himself, these refused to see in her just the same Charlotte the old ones had seen. The transformation was dispiriting to her; it was not enlivening to him. He felt that she could not be to him what she had been; she was hurt by his comparative aloofness, she was piqued by his regrets for Italy.

Goethe was still a young man; indeed, he never grew old. In his latter years could be applied to him the saying of Solon: "I am always learning ; only by that do I perceive that I am growing older." A man of thirty-nine is younger than a woman of thirty-nine, and Charlotte was forty-six. Women there are who, like some men, grow not old with years. With both, this is probably an effect of temperament and moral structure more than of intellect. Morose people, very selfish people, cannot keep their youth. People who overfeed grow old sooner than others ; and yet, to keep young is a matter of mind more than of body. Charlotte was not old for her years, but she had not the vivacity to keep younger than her years.

Goethe's notes to Charlotte are much less frequent and less warm than before his departure for Italy. He preserves *du*, but it is now the *du* of long friendship. From going to Kochberg he excuses himself on account of the weather. The social circle of Weimar seems to have been put out of tune by the *Maestro* being uncomfortable. At a ball he paid no attention to married ladies, but danced the whole evening with the *Frauleins*. With Herder's wife Goethe was always excellent friends. In the middle of August he invited her and Charlotte's sister Imhoff to tea. I told him, writes Mad. Herder, that I would come if Charlotte von Stein came with us. "Ah! with her, nothing is to be done," said Goethe, "she is out of humor." Knebel writes to Lottchen : "Goethe is not so unhappy in Weimar as people think. He is clear-headed, and knows that the past should be looked upon as a dream ; and yet it is a very painful feeling for him to have lost the confidence of his old friend Charlotte, who had been so much to him."

About this time Imhoff died in Munich, whereupon Goethe writes to Charlotte at Kochberg : "Your sister is much grieved. She will discover by and by that it is for her happiness that he is gone." On the fifth of September, Goethe, with Fritz, Frau von Schardt, and Herder's wife, drove together to Kochberg, where, according to Mad. Herder, he was received by Charlotte without cordiality. This put him out of tune the whole day. He showed them drawings. In the afternoon he went to sleep. In the evening he spoke much of Herder and his views of Christianity, against which he expressed himself very strongly. Another day they all drove to Rudolstadt ; and there Goethe first met Schiller.

To a lively letter from her little sister-in-law, giving an account of public and private doings in Weimar, Charlotte wrote in answer on the

eighteenth of September: "You have no doubt
heard that I have been in Jena. Knebel is not
contented. He lacks hope and expectation.
Yet, happy is he that he still strives after hope
and expectation:—

> The autumn strips the grove,
> And winter's frost becomes my hope.

"Now I will take a drive, for the quiet roads
here are good for hypochondria. Next week I
go to Rudolstadt. Last week the Lengefelds
were with me and also Schiller; he seems to
me to be a right good man, with whom it is
pleasant to go about. This is all my news.
Farewell. Greet all in the parental house,
Waldner and the Egloffsteins."

In the beginning of October, Knebel spent
a few days at Kochberg, and, as if to complete
the sketch of Charlotte he had sent to his
sister a short time before, writes to her as follows: "She is an admirable woman, and lives
in a clear serenity, which, with her sensitive,
refined nature, takes the place of warmth. Her
mind is of the intellectual type, and yet she
has none of the pretension of intellect. She
says she must, one of these days, live a while
with you, and that she looks forward to as a
great happiness. She thinks her sister Imhoff

lives only by instinct, yet she is very fond of her."

Some days later Charlotte carried off with her Lottchen von Lengefeld from Rudolstadt to Kochberg. Schiller and Lottchen were attracted to each other, and on Schiller's complaining to her that Frau von Stein knew how to make her sojourn in the country very agreeable by robbing other people, Lottchen answers : " I am perfectly well here and enjoy intercourse with the dear Stein. She is a noble woman, and has so many agreeable talents. I am reading here a pleasant book of travels through Greece." Schiller rejoins : " Enjoy your very fine days in Kochberg. You are in very good hands. I have become attached to the Frau von Stein since I have seen more of her. I admire the beautiful earnestness of her character ; she takes an interest in what she believes to be true, and what is noble. Many people die, without ever having had any thought hereof. In you, too, I love this mingling of liveliness and earnestness."

How capable Goethe was of a purely platonic love for a superior attractive woman, has been shown by his ten years' devotion to Charlotte von Stein, — a devotion unprecedented in biography, and, in a man of his erotic susceptibility, almost incredible. Had Charlotte been kinder to him on his return from Italy, had she borne herself towards him with more sympathy and less exaction, with more softness and less assumption, one cannot say but that the old relation would have been resumed with much of its old cordiality. That she did not seek to win him back by gentleness and tenderness, if it proves a certain want in her of finest feminine quality, of the deeper sensibility, proves, at the same time, that she was not an artful woman. Had she possessed more depth of passion or more craft, she would not have forced Goethe into that disappointed, sore state of feeling which left him open to temptation from youthful beauty, temptation, to which during the ten years of devotion to her he had probably been more than once exposed, but had never yielded. Then, his heart was kept faithful through a warmth nourished by her reciprocation and her womanly sympathy. Now, her want of sympathy, her coldness, had suddenly chilled that glow, already weakened by absence and distance but by no means extinguished.

Goethe had not been at home many weeks when he was one day timidly accosted in the park by a young girl with a petition to obtain

a place for Vulpius, the well known author of
robber-tales, among them "Rinaldo Rinaldini,"
which we read sixty years ago. The bringer
of the petition was the sister of Vulpius, Christiane, described by Madame Schopenhauer, says
Lewes, as being then a blooming girl, with
small, graceful figure, golden-brown locks, rosy
lips, and laughing eyes. To Goethe, sighing
for Italy, here was an Hesperian apparition to
delight his eye in the Hyperborean gloom of
Thuringia, a glowing materialization of the
sunny, sensuous south. He surrendered himself to the unexpected fascination, and Christiane surrendered herself to him.

In a small town such an affair could not be
long concealed, especially when involving its
most distinguished inhabitant, and he just
then, from his recent return home, the observed of all observers. It soon came to the
ears of Charlotte. Having seen into what an
unjustifiable state of offense she had been
thrown without cause, we can infer the condition of her feelings now that she had ground
for reproach. That there had been scenes between them, before the affair with Christiane
came to light, is evident from the subjoined
letter from Goethe to Charlotte. This letter,
dated June 1st, 1789, shows not only how un-

reasonable and injudicious she had been, but how imperious and unrelenting.

"I thank thee for the letter thou leftst for me, although it troubled me in more ways than one. I delayed answering it, because in such a case it is difficult to be sincere and not give pain.

"How much I love thee, how fully I know my duty towards thee and Fritz, I have shown by my return from Italy. I were there still had I conformed to the duke's wish; Herder went thither, and as I did not foresee that I could do anything for the crown-prince, I had scarcely anything else in my thought but thee and Fritz.

"What I left behind in Italy I will not now repeat; my confidence in regard to that, thou hast received in an unfriendly way.

"Unhappily, when I arrived, thou wast in a peculiar mood, and I acknowledge that the manner in which you received me was exceedingly painful to me. I saw Herder and the duchess set out, with an empty place in the carriage urgently offered to me; I stayed for the sake of those friends for whom I had come, and this, when I was pertinaciously told that I might just as well have stayed away, that I took no interest in people, and so forth.

And all this before there could have been any
word about the affair which seems so to grieve
thee.,

"And what is this affair? Who is robbed
by it? Who has a claim on the feelings I give
the poor creature? Who on the hours I pass
with her?

" Ask Fritz, ask the Herders, ask any one
who knows me intimately, whether I am less
sympathetic, less active, or less friendly than
before? Whether I do not rather now, for the
first time, rightly belong to them and to society?

"And it must be by a miracle if the best,
the most intimate relation of all, that to thee,
should have ceased.

" How vividly I have felt that this relation
still exists when I have found thee disposed to
talk with me on interesting subjects.

"But this I acknowledge, that the manner
in which you have treated me hitherto I cannot
endure. When I was inclined to talk, you shut
my lips ; when communicative about Italy you
reproached me with indifference ; when active
for my friends, with coldness and neglect of
you. You criticised my every look, found fault
with my movements, my way of life, and put me
ill at ease. How can openness and confidence

thrive, if you repulse me with predetermined ill-humor?

"I should like to add more, did I not fear that in thy present mood it would irritate rather than conciliate thee.

"Unhappily, thou hast long despised my advice in regard to coffee, and adopted a regimen highly injurious to thy health. As though it were not already difficult enough to overcome certain moral impressions, thou strengthenest the hypochondriacal tormenting power of gloomy imaginations through a physical means, the injurious effects of which thou for a time acknowledgest, gavest up for a while, and foundst thyself better. May the cure and the journey do thee good. I don't entirely give up the hope that thou wilt again know me for what I am. Farewell. Fritz is happy and visits me constantly. The prince is well and lively."

What a letter! How characteristic of Goethe, of his gentleness, of his frankness, of his truth of soul! It is, too, a revelation: it opens to us interiors. It shows what Goethe had to bear on his arrival from Italy. He was paying the exquisite penalty of genius, which is ever discovering new enriching solitudes, into which the less gifted cannot at first tread, but whose wealth genius, with its divine communicativeness, longs to share with others.

At the top of this letter Charlotte von Stein wrote, " O ! ! ! " Was this an O ! of lamentation or of indignation ?

Charlotte being what she was, a comparatively passionless woman, a proud, an intellectual, and at the same time an affectionate woman, who had held Goethe bethralled for so many years, for her to have a devoted lover, and one so eminent, snatched away by an obscure girl, who was nothing but what the Italians call *un bel pezzo di carne* (a fine piece of flesh), was indeed a severe trial. Her influence over Goethe had been absolute and exceptional, especially grateful to her, who was even unusually fond of power, this exercise of it most gratifying to any woman. What an irrepressible desire most of us have to direct, to rule, other people. Is this from an unconscious, profound, continuous sympathy with our fellow-men, that secretly moves us to endeavor to absorb them into ourselves ? Or is it from the less elevated feeling that is ever urging us to get our neighbors' lots and lands into our inclosure ?

Had Goethe been "a piece of perfection," he would not have had the affair with Christiane ;

and had Charlotte been "a piece of perfection" she would not have taken that affair so indignantly to heart. For one, I cannot but say that I am glad they were not. "Pieces of perfection" are not human : they belong to a different genus from ourselves : they are out of the range of our sympathies. We prefer beings who, passion-stirred, are at times passion-mastered. Such as these are more prolific material for human life, for human literature. When, through the mists of error from overpowering feeling, there shines a rock-set pharos, kept ever alight by moral and religious principle, they are sure to be guided through these temporary storms ; and while we love them the more for their warm, impulsive humanity, we deeply respect them for, and are ourselves strengthened by, their ultimate self-subjection to duty.

As the moral law comes out of man's interior, even in the presence of the highest standard, — which we should ever strive to elevate by sounding the deepest, truest, completest natures, — in the presence of this standard, and by virtue of its very elevation, some range should be given to individual constitution, and especially should allowance be made for richness and fullness of endowment. To do this is but to practice that charity which is the first of virtues, because, having no relation to self, it is a calm current of disinterested love towards others ; and if to charity be added diffidence in judging our neighbor, any but the self-righteous will pause before venturing to condemn Goethe, one who never sought to profit himself by the loss of others, a man with an intellect clear and strong, broad and penetrating, diverse and solid, with sensibilities deep, active, watchful, ever urging him to seek the true and the good and the beautiful, those spiritualizing energies of the human mind. Goethe was so great and worthy that he should be permitted to be a law unto himself, — a man from whom other men can learn the law, and to whom few, very few, of the sons of the earth are pure and high enough to teach the higher things, and none pure and high enough to pass judgment upon him.

Let us take Goethe as he was, — one of the supreme men of the race, — and not presume to wish him other than he was. Look clearly into him, — you cannot look clearly into a man without sympathy, — and you will behold a being who is, in the highest sense, representative of humanity. By studying him, without venturing to judge him, we shall deepen our insight

into him, into nature, into ourselves. But
above all, let no one try to get a view of
Goethe through the dimness shed by a pharisaical, unsavory lamp, unsavory, because fed
with bad oil, or rather with the foul grease
that has been gathered by conceit out of the
fragments of an ineffectual life, of a life of pretension and worldliness. Before Goethe, a
man who was never mastered by the passions
of envy or jealousy or hatred or covetousness
or ambition, —any one of which leads to manifold chronic immoralities, — the healthy attitude in which to stand is an attitude of sympathy, of modesty, of deference, of reverence ;
and thus standing, a glow of admiration and
gratitude will melt his errors into vapor that
will cast no shadow upon our hearts, which
have been otherwise strengthened and purified
by his wisdom and his poetry, and by his high
example of ceaseless aspiration. Goethe was a
great man, a man of truth and heart, a good
man, one of the most moral, most religious
men that ever lived. In his life there was a
daily beauty, created and kept ever fresh by
his uprightness and his active, inexhaustible
kindness.

13

XV.

IN Charlotte's heart there was a void, an aching void. The breach with Goethe, his defection, as she called it, was a twofold evil, an outward loss of distinction in the world, and an inward distress. Instead of smiling, cordial imaginations of him when he was absent, instead of always welcoming thought of him as the dearest guest of silent, lonely hours, she had to repel, to strive to exclude, all thoughts of him ; for now these were not laden with balm, but bore every one a sting, a sting to her affections, a sting to her pride. The memory of him, which she could not banish, which used to be a joy, was now a grief. Had he only cooled towards her, she might hope to rekindle his feelings (to be sure the way she treated him when he first returned from Italy was as injudicious as it was unjust), but he had warmed towards another, and that with a profane love. The thought of Christiane embittered still her bitter draught.

Her unhappiness was aggravated by the want of sympathy in some of her friends. Herder's wife and Frau von Kalb sided with Goethe. She thought the Duchess Louise neglected her, and she wrote her a letter of complaint, which Louise answered in her clear, sweet way. Charlotte had a resource in Lottchen and Schiller to whom Lottchen was about to be married. In the flush of this pleasant excitement, her husband fell ill and required her constant attention.

Charlotte and others made strong efforts to get Schiller a place. The duke granted him a pension, but it was at first a small one of only two hundred dollars. Goethe had lent his influence to obtain for him a professorship in Jena, but it was a professorship without salary. Lottchen, in a letter from Weimar to Schiller, relates that she had had a narrow escape from an awkward speech. Charlotte, giving warm expression to her attachment to Schiller and herself, said that were she to lose her husband she should go and live with them in Jena, at which Lottchen exclaimed, "Oh!" but bethought her just in time to hold in an exclamation of "joy at the death of poor papa Stein."

The French Revolution, beginning to show

its bloody side, made further divisions in the circle, the duchess, Charlotte, and Goethe deploring the whole movement, Herder and Knebel exulting in it. Over them all a sudden gloom was thrown by a suicide, a brother of Knebel having shot himself within a few paces of Knebel. At this period Goethe had ceased writing to Charlotte, and thus concludes, in March, 1790, a letter to Fritz: "Greet thy father and mother, and love me, as I shall always love and value thee." In company Charlotte and Goethe met on the footing of ordinary politeness. In answer to a letter from Charlotte, her unswerving friend, the Duchess Louise, writes to her to Kochberg: "I think often of you, my dear Stein, and do you likewise remember me when you have nothing better to think of. You heard a sermon on Sunday which, you say, wearied you; and I heard one from Herder, which was of an extraordinary kind. He said some very fine things, and others quite ordinary. He broke forth strongly against people for not reading often enough the church-hymns, complained that only mechanics and peasants read them. He sharply condemned teas and cakes, and let fly generally against lavishness and vanity; he declared, at the same time, that there must be in the world differences of rank, but that no one need envy those of higher rank, because they were born with many prejudices, from which they have difficulty in freeing themselves. You see he remains true to his habits. . . . . Your husband will tell you what is going on here; but I will say no more than what I have so often said, that I love you with my whole heart, my dear Stein, and that I shall love you all my life. I beg you leave off hereafter in your letters *Madame* and *your most obedient.*"

Before the year ended, Charlotte had to comfort her mother on account of the death of the old Court-marshal von Schardt, who, after confinement to the house for many years, was still, at the age of eighty, unwilling to quit the earth. To Lottchen she writes that she is reading Schiller's "Thirty Years' War" to the duchess, with great enjoyment to both, although the duchess had read it once before; and she adds: "Would that Schiller had a ducat for every syllable of it."

Troubles multiplied upon Charlotte. Her eldest son got into difficulty at the court of Meclenburg, where he had a good post; hypochondria was part of her husband's malady; Fritz was about to leave her for Jena, as student

in the University. The French Revolution
continued to make discord among friends. The
sister of Knebel, a superior woman, was appointed governess to the duke's daughter, the
Princess Caroline, and one evening, Knebel
having taken her to see Charlotte, Knebel and
Charlotte got into so warm a discussion on
politics, that Charlotte's sister thought she
would have boxed his ears, and his own sister
wished that she had done so.

In the mean time Goethe had been blessed
with what to him was as lively a joy as to
women, — the birth of a son. He took Christiane into his house. "Good society," with its
conventional morality, howled, not being able
to perceive that, in doing thus, he had done
the truly honest thing. In defying high-bred
usage, Goethe showed his manliness, his humanity, his sense of duty. He took Christiane
to his home as his wife. He loved her, and
she loved him. He felt that he and Christiane
were more really husband and wife than were
his friends Stein and Charlotte. To enter into
formal matrimony he had probably not felt encouraged by the matrimonial prosperity around
him of the Steins, the Imhoffs, the De Kalbs,
the duke and duchess.

Goethe was not one who talked virtue and

acted vice. His nature was thoroughly truthful; there was not a particle of hypocrite in him. Some of those who cried out against him might possibly have been benefited by studying the character of Angelo in "Measure for Measure." The self-seeking, the calculating, the shallow-hearted are often quick to pass sentence on the full-souled; as though a man, addicted to circumvention, and cheating within the limits of the law, should swell with assumed superiority over, and with indignant moral condemnation of, a neighbor, who, under strong provocation, had, in a fit of passion, knocked a man down with his fist. Herder christened Goethe's boy, the duke standing by as god-father.

Goethe took Christiane to his home, where she lived with him for twenty-eight years until her death, for the last ten in legal wedlock. That this was not earlier was owing to herself. For a fuller statement, the reader is referred to the writer's volume, "Goethe, his Life and Works." The translation there first published, is here repeated of Goethe's exquisite little poem, which in his happiest lyrical vein illustrates the taking of Christiane to his home.

FOUND.

I roamed at random
　Athrough a wood,
To seek for nothing —
　That was my mood.

I did in shadow
　A floweret spy ;
As stars 't was lustrous,
　Or a wee eye.

I wished to break it ;
　Then soft it said :
Shall I be broken
　Quickly to fade?

With all its rootlets,
　Dug from the loam,
To my own garden
　I bore it home.

In a still corner
　I gave it room ;
And there it thriveth,
　Ever in bloom.

Charlotte continued to be unhappy ; and in
her case, as in all cases, her unhappiness came
from within herself. The soul is paramount,
and makes its own heaven or hell. The more
complete the self-sacrifice, the fuller and higher
will be the heaven on earth. Charlotte was
capable of self-denial ; she was at this time de-

nying herself for her friends, her children, her
husband; but she was not capable of that degree of self-sacrifice which would have made
her subdue pride and would have spiritualized
her affection. Had she been, in place of the
jealousy that caused hatred of Goethe's new
joy in the company of another woman, she
would have felt sympathy for him, and her own
heart-ache would have been changed almost
into gladness. Could she have effaced the
lower self, the self that would still hold Goethe
in thrall against the tendency of his own being,
her higher self, thus asserting its supremacy,
would have quenched all her suffering. Is any
one capable of such disinterestedness? At all
events, she was not, and thence her days were
dogged by a phantom, evoked out of her own
egoism, and which a strong exercise of virtue
would have rebuked and laid. Her love for
Goethe was not quite so pure as she believed
it to be; there was in it an egotistic despotism
that would subject him to her. It was not of
that angelic quality that is busied solely with
the wishes and the well-being of its object. If,
in the sacrifice of one's self to friends, to children, to husband, there is a large self-gratification, the sacrifice of one's desire to appropriate
the love of another would bring a larger, sweeter

self-gratification. There is no higher, surer law than that to go out of one's self, to efface one's self, for the sake of another, yields the richest, healthiest fruit of which earthly life is capable.

When Herder wrote of Goethe, who had accompanied the duke to the siege of Mayence, that he had grown "young and corpulent," Charlotte's bitter comment, that he was rolling in sensual well-being and had foregone his higher ideal aims, had in it a self-righteousness of which she was entirely unconscious. In honorable contrast to this grossness she held up fleshless Schiller! Poor Schiller! how he would have leapt with joy to find himself getting fleshy like Goethe. Nor let the reader assume that I am too hard upon my dear heroine. She has my sympathy even in her own least ideal moods ; only she was not " a piece of perfection." That in former years, before the bond between her and Goethe was broken, she had been pricked by the thorns while enjoying the rose, had been gnawed by the perplexing passion of jealousy, may be inferred from a sentence in a note to Lottchen, did we not already know from the individualities of herself and Goethe that it must have been so. She says to Lottchen : " You are also my only lover of whom I never had any suspicion." Then it was temporary discomfort, springing from doubt, from the "forgeries of jealousy;" now it was permanent misery, jealousy most unexpectedly, most hideously consummated.

A little later she had from Lottchen a joyful piece of news. The way in which it acted on her bears lively witness to her devotion to her friends. The news is worth recording here, that we may do honor to the prince who caused it by an act which lifts his name high on the roll of "aristocrats," and binds it to that of the immortal Schiller. Charlotte writes: "I had a headache: I had risen in bad spirits: now I have read your letter, all is gone; I should like to fly to you, were I sure of my health and the weather." Lottchen's letter told her that the Prince of Augustenburg had offered Schiller a thousand dollars a year for three years until his health should be restored.

The following glimpse of Herder lays bare this distinguished man's weak side, of which his best friends, especially the duchess and Goethe, had often cause to complain, and shows, at the same time, the humane liberality of the Weimar court, that bore with disagreeable weaknesses so kindly. The Duchess Louise writes to Charlotte: "I expect to dinner the coadjutor (Dalberg), and have invited to

meet him our genial spirits, also Herder, in the
hope that he will be less crabbed than he was
last Friday, when I had him to dinner and he
was quite unbearable ; for six months I have
not seen him in so bad a humor ; he spoke
only in monosyllables, and all his rancor against
the nobility was aroused.   Verily, he will have
to write a third part to his new work on the
'Advancement of Humanity.'"

There was yet no abatement of Charlotte's
bitterness against Goethe. He did not visit
her, choosing not to expose himself to her re-
proaches, and when they met in company he
had little to say to her.   In November, 1793,
she writes to Fritz : " Goethe has now a little
daughter, too, at which he is excessively delighted ; for he is as friendly as an ear-wig,
makes French puns, and himself stood god-
father to the little child."   Had we not so
many witnesses to Charlotte's goodness of
heart, and such evidence in her letters to, and
conduct towards, her friends of affectionate
sympathy, we might be misled to believe in
the hardness of her nature, when we find her
bosom so closed against all tenderness for
Goethe's parental instinct.   She who had
known what it is "to love the babe that
milks me," how could she not have had some

fellow-feeling for her old lover in his paternal rapture, a rapture so intense that when, a few weeks later, he lost this little daughter, he wept aloud and threw himself in agony on the floor. And of what undying interest is this touching fact to all the civilized world, which hereby gains a look into that deep spring of sensibility, to whose overflow it owes some of its richest poetic inheritance.

In the same letter she describes to Fritz (at Hamburg) the weekly round of entertainments at Weimar : " Court on Sundays ; Wednesdays at the duchess mother's ; dancing club every other Friday ; Mondays at the duchess mother's meeting of the wits and authors, a kind of academy where they draw, read, and drink champagne." She tells Fritz she is very desirous of seeing the Hamburg theater, and also the movement of a large commercial town, of which she has no conception.

When Goethe reopened the mines of Ilmenau, he invited his friends to take shares. The mines had not been successful, and the shares had fallen greatly in value. Charlotte writes to Fritz that she had just sold four shares at a reduced price, and adds : " I am sorry to say, I have no longer faith in anything our departed friend has a hand in ; he must surely have offended his guardian-spirit, and has no more luck."

And now came bad news from the frontier; the Prussian army had been repulsed. At the end of November Charlotte writes to Fritz: "And one can see no end to it all; unless some Gustavus or Bernard were again to rise up; and who knows if even these would have the strength; for it is the first time since the world was that the devil carries on war against the nations." On the sixth of December she writes to Lottchen: "I am very glad that no one very near to my heart is in the war; I do not understand how any one can bear it. Is Schiller at last convinced about the French Revolution, and may I now call the National Convention robbers, without his being amazed as he once was? I am glad he is a German; otherwise he would have been guillotined long since; for, wherever there is a noble drop of blood, that they shed."

On the twenty-sixth of December, 1793, died Charlotte's husband, Baron von Stein. Charlotte wrote: "He looked beautiful in death. All that was unpleasant in his countenance, — caused by the mental malady which vexed him and others, — a gentle death had brought again into rest, and restored his fine equilibrium."

XVI.

In 1794 began the intimate literary and personal union between Goethe and Schiller. Through Charlotte's friendship for Schiller and his wife there was some renewal of friendly relations between her and Goethe. About this time, Goethe, who always held affectionately to Fritz, had it in his power to be of service to him. Indeed Charlotte herself encouraged Fritz to rely upon Goethe; for, notwithstanding her hard speeches about him, she knew how trustworthy he was, and how kind and true a friend.

The French Revolution, with its astounding progress and power, was more and more busying people's thoughts, saddening them with vague fears. Even among those who recognized its wholesome office as cleanser of accumulated foulness in church and state, few could discern, behind its crimes and extravagances, the light of regeneration which, unknown to the actors in the tempestuous movement, was guiding them and their passions towards a healthier, higher state. Terror was the feeling of neighboring nations. People's thoughts of the future were darkened by a strange dread. In midsummer of 1794, Charlotte put into a letter to Lottchen these prophetic words : " Your feelings about the war are very sound ; I fear we shall yet all be swallowed up by the French." And a few days later, she makes on Robespierre this comment, which has been since often and easily uttered from the calm, remote height of retrospection, but to make which in the hot presence of 1794 shows a rare insight into the situation : " The fate of Robespierre was not unexpected to me ; I regard it as a matter of course that these abominations of humanity must devour one another."

Of the progress made towards a better feeling in regard to Goethe through Fritz, the following sentence in a letter to him is a token : " This morning early, Goethe sent me a letter from thee to him to read, with the request to inclose to thee the accompanying note." What probably somewhat contributed to this progress was the agreement in opinion between Charlotte and Goethe on the French Revolution. In his Diary of this year Goethe wrote : " Robespierre's atrocities had appalled the world, and the sense of joy was so lost that no one trusted himself to shout at his downfall." In the same letter to Fritz, from which the sentence above is quoted, Charlotte wrote : " On the tenth of September the court goes to Eisenach for six weeks and then I to Kochberg to thy brother. If the weather continues good, I shall enjoy it. Who knows but this is the last time that we shall dwell together in peace; for the French or French principles will at last turn the world into a wide desert and haunt of murder." In the same letter she tells Fritz of the divorce of Beulwitz from his wife, who was the sister of Lottchen, Beulwitz to marry a lady of Meiningen, and she her cousin von Wollzogen.

Lottchen had confided to Charlotte that Goethe's "Roman Elegies" were to be published in Schiller's new monthly literary journal, " The Hours," and that, from a poetical point of view, they were admirable. To which Charlotte answers : " The well-known Eligies I have often heard praised, but my former friend probably did not think me worthy enough to give them to me. He wished to publish them some years ago, but the duke advised him against it. How our gracious lord was just for a moment overcome by this pedantic moral susceptibility, is to me incomprehensible." She evidently supposed

these Elegies to have been writen in Rome and
to have referred to Goethe's Italian loves. But
it was even worse with them than that. Goethe
having for years ceased to make Charlotte his
poetical confidant, would surely not have resumed the practice by imparting to her poems
which, professedly Roman, were written in
Weimar, and were nevertheless pagan-Cattullian
in spirit, and for which Christiane had been the
inspiration. That is a lively characteristic fling
at her friend, the duke, who had stood god-
father to Goethe's first-born.

In this year Charlotte finished her drama
of "Dido," left in manuscript to her friend
Lottchen, the wife of Schiller, and first published in 1867 from the manuscript in possession of the Baroness von Gleichen-Russ-
wurm, daughter of Schiller and Lottchen, and
with consent of Baron von Stein-Kochberg,
grandson of Charlotte von Stein. "Dido"
was apparently written under a pressure similar to that which brought into being Goethe's
"Werther," wherewith he gave salutary vent to
feelings and thoughts that were torturing his
heart and threatening him with suicide. Charlotte was far from any suicidal tendency, but
she was self-tormented, and, attributing to
Goethe her unhappy condition, which was due

to her own want of moral discipline, she sought some relief in caricaturing Goethe under the name of *Orgo*, who is represented as a selfish, sensual poet and faithless lover. As a literary work the drama is mediocre. Bitterness is not a spring of inspiration, and "Dido" is not lively as caricature. It hardly does justice to Charlotte's literary capacity, and is only a memorial of a woman's exaggerated jealousy, which makes her unjust to the man she had once loved and esteemed, whom she continued to esteem in spite of herself, and to whom, through his love for her, she had been, as he called her, a guardian-spirit for ten years.

That Charlotte, by writing "Dido," had not got rid of all the "perilous stuff" that oppressed her is too apparent from her letters. In the beginning of 1796 she spent several days at Jena, and on a visit to the Schillers, as she was about to take leave, Goethe came in. "I had not seen him for several months," she writes to Fritz; "he was horribly stout, with short arms, and kept his hands thrust into his trowsers' pockets. Schiller beside him looked like a heavenly genius. His health was tolerable, and the pale calmness on his countenance made him interesting. I should like to know if to Goethe I seem as much changed in appearance as he does to me. He has come to be thoroughly of the earth, from which we are taken. Poor Goethe, who was once so fond of us."

When Goethe returned to Weimar he did not go to see Charlotte, as on his last visit, as well as when they met at Schiller's, she had made herself disagreeable to him. A little later she had Lottchen to stay with her, while Schiller lodged with Goethe. Goethe's little son, August, came often to her house to play with Schiller's Carl. Charlotte writes to Fritz: " He seems to be a good child. I gave him some playthings, which made him very happy, and after three several pauses, in which he seemed to be counting the presents in his little head, he uttered emphatically, ' I thank you.' I can at times perceive in him separately the distinguished nature of the father and the commoner one of the mother." The duchess went to see her, accompanied by Schiller. The evening before, she and Schiller " disputed themselves tired on the human race, which it seems to him possible to improve, to me not. At last he had to admit that human nature cannot be changed, but that the striving for something higher is proper to man." On another trip to Jena she made the acquaintance of A. W. Schlegel, whom she calls " a very endurable man." On returning to Weimar, she writes to Lottchen: "I was rejoiced to see Schiller looking so well. Greet him cordially from me, and, if you think proper, give also to the stout privy councilor (Goethe) a good evening in my name."

Goethe felt how much disappointment and pain he had caused Charlotte, and with his affectionate, gentle nature, wearied not, in the face of her rebuffs, and her unkind speeches about him, in trying to conciliate one to whom he had been so long devoted, his obligations to whom he cordially acknowledged, and whose mind and character he highly prized. One day in June, as Charlotte was sitting in her favorite summer seat under the orange-trees before her house (where the Duchess Louise came often to sit and chat with her), Goethe with his little August passed that way, and on her invitation took a seat beside her, and by his bearing and talk so subdued her now chronic dissatisfaction with him that, in relating the incident to Lottchen, she said, " It is inconceivable to me how he could ever have become to me so much a stranger." But the good impression was not lasting. Two or three months later, she and the duchess, going into the sick-room of the duke, found Goethe there, who seemed disconcerted, so that the duchess was troubled ; " but I," she wrote, " who have no longer any respect for men of genius (*schoene geister*), rattled away about all sorts of things, and made the hour pass off lightly." Here is a glimpse of an interesting feature of her mind. At this period she was anxious about Fritz, who wished to enter the service of Prussia, in order to have a wider field. She writes to Fritz : " Last night, as I was about to go to sleep, I begged my guardian spirit to tell me something of thy good or bad fortune ; for he has been so kind as to do this for me more than once. But on awaking I found in my head nothing but a dry computation."

Goethe's last letter to Charlotte was dated the eighth of June, 1789, a few days after that painful significant one over which she wrote "O!" His next, after a silent interval of more than seven years, is dated September the seventh, 1796. Fritz and his prospects are the subject of it, and it ends with this touching paragraph : " Farewell ; allow me when I return (from Jena) to speak further on this subject. Allow, moreover, my poor boy to be made happy in your presence, and to form himself in your looks. Of how kind you have been to him I cannot think without emotion."

Had she not quarreled with Goethe (he never quarreled with her) she would not have condemned the epigrammatic war which he and Schiller were at this time waging against their assailants. The shooting up of two such brilliant stars into the literary empyrean, which they were gladdening with a new illumination, made all the eyes of impotent pretension to wink with pain. Disappointed, ambitious, jealous mediocrities were all astir to extinguish or bedim these genial luminaries who, they felt, would disperse the twilight in which alone themselves could thrive. These attacks the two Weimar friends met with the weapons most effective in such cases, — with witty ridicule and playful satire in the shape of caustic distichs, which they discharged by scores at their writhing assailants.

With Schiller even Charlotte was somewhat put out, casting upon him some of her dissatisfaction with his great friend, so that she did not wholly except him from her general denunciation of men of genius who, as a class, she erringly thought, care little about morality, but follow the bent of their ambitious natures. So blinded was she by her morbid feeling towards Goethe that she would not acknowledge that the pages of the deeper poets are mines of the richest moral treasures.

Weimar had grown to be an intellectual focus to superior minds. This summer appeared there one of those men of power whose writings have in them life enough long to survive the hand that wrote them. This was the large-souled Jean Paul Richter. A reception was given him at Frau von Kalb's, where was assembled all that was most cultivated. Only Schiller (who still resided in Jena) and Goethe were not present. By Richter's eccentricity (albeit a natural and a genial eccentricity) and his want of form as artist, they were too much repelled to do justice to the intellectual grasp, the deep, broad humanity, the humor and fresh wisdom of the good and great Richter. Schiller, after an interview with him, said he was an extraordinary phenomenon. To Goethe, the true, noble Richter bore no grudge for not valuing him. In his work on Æsthetics he speaks of Goethe as one who at times reached the highest excellence. Varnhagen von Ense, in his diary records a conversation with Richter at his home in Baireuth in 1808 : " Of Goethe he said, 'Goethe is a consecrated head; he has a place of his own high above us all.' We spoke of Goethe afterwards, for some time : Jean Paul with more and more admiration, nay, with a sort of fear and awe-struck reverence." Besides Richter, the Humboldts, two genuine "aristocrats," paid a visit to Weimar about this time.

That Charlotte's feelings towards Goethe were getting into a healthier state is shown by her having dined at his house, in a large company, in the early part of 1797. This year her beloved Fritz became a twofold source of anxiety. He had not only given up his post in Weimar before he was sure of another in Prussia, but, in his letter of resignation to the duke, he had very improperly said that the Weimar service was without honor. This expression had offended the duchess so deeply that it caused a temporary coolness between her and Charlotte. At the same time Fritz was thinking of a marriage which she could not approve of. By these troubles her frequent headaches were aggravated. She wrote to Fritz: " Thou hast a good, noble friend in Frau von Maltzan, and he, too, pleases me. Let the two be thy advisers, and sacrifice thy happiness rather than do any thing that shall lower thee morally. Thou hast been my ideal of a pure, beautiful soul: I should like to take it as it is with me into the grave."

Goethe, who was doing what he could to reconcile Charlotte to the inevitable, sent her on

her birthday, by his little August, a large al-
mond cake and a copy of his recently published
poem, " Hermann and Dorothea," superbly
bound, with a silver clasp. Other friends called
on that day to offer their congratulations,
among them the duke. The following incident proves how much she was respected by
her ducal friends, while it is another illustra-
tion of her high spirit, and also of the duke's
occasional hastiness, and at the same time of
his substantial amiability. He proposed to her
a walk in the hall, in the course of which he
mentioned his displeasure that her son Carl
should have appeared at court without a " hair-
bag," to which she answered somewhat sharply,
and then left him. The duke and duchess sent
Charlotte's sister-in-law to her to beg her not
to say any thing to Carl about it, and that the
duke had no intention of offending her.

The next year she witnessed the formal be-
trothal of her son Carl to Amalia von Seebach, a match which she cordially approved.
In April she reports to Fritz a great breakfast
at Goethe's: "I have just come from a grand
breakfast at Goethe's, who wished to honor by
a high company his elegant rooms adorned
with the fine arts. All our princely personages were there, and the crown-prince of Gotha,

and many ladies." Nevertheless she could not withhold herself from giving her host a hit harmless in comparison with some she had been in the habit of giving him. The distinguished actor Iffland had a very homely wife, whereupon she remarked, that great artists seemed not to desire to have in their halves the noble and beautiful poetry of nature. And a little later she writes : " I see Goethe seldom, and when I do see him I am alarmed at his increasing stoutness."

Few persons are generously warm enough, especially after middle life, to radiate warmth upon their fellows. Charlotte was not one of these few. The daily feeling of disappointment and indifference, generated by centering one's thoughts too habitually upon the self, threatened to grow upon her as she advanced towards old age. She was not capable of that daily self-forgetting which is the best source of cheerfulness and content. Against this benumbing tendency she struggled, as the following passage in a note to Lottchen seems to show: " Resignation has been with me too often repeated, and I have grown more indifferent to life and the business of life than I could wish. You and the Duchess Louise hold me solely through your love, and many a time

I am puzzled to know how it is that you still
love me, and should like much to twine something agreeable into your lives."

The autumn of this year was signalized by
the bringing out upon the Weimar stage of the
first part of Schiller's greatest tragedy, "Wallenstein." To be present at the rehearsal of
"Wallenstein's camp," Schiller came from
Jena. Goethe showed the liveliest interest in
its success, as did Charlotte, for the sake of
Schiller's wife, Lottchen.

Charlotte continued anxious about Fritz and
his prospects, public and matrimonial. Towards
the end of the year she wrote him this maternal letter : " I think much of thee, and am
often sad that I am so entirely separated from
thee without thy fortune being in the least
improved thereby. Let no wife be put upon
thee, that thou mightest hereafter deplore. I
am afraid thou mightest be deceived in regard
to a wife as in regard to a post. I have observed that thou, good soul, art credulous.
Forgive me ; I would not give thee pain, dear,
good Fritz, and so far away, where it cannot
quickly be made good again. Thou hast
written to Amelia (Imhoff) a letter which made
her weep. The fault of pretension, with which
thou didst reproach her somewhat roughly,

were it even possible to lay aside, with it would disappear all the virtues and talents that depend on it." Scarcely was this letter dispatched than the mother's anxiety was dispelled, for news came that Fritz was appointed councilor in the war and domain department of Prussia.

In this cousin of Fritz, Charlotte's niece Amelia, to whom he had written the chiding letter, Charlotte took a growing interest, on account of her literary promise. Amelia had just finished a poem with which her aunt was much pleased, and of which Goethe thought so well that he hoped to get her for it from his publisher one thousand *thaler*, the sum he received for "Herman and Dorothea."

The last year of the century opened cheerfully for Charlotte. Schiller and his wife came to pass several weeks in Weimar, where "The Piccolomini" (second part of "Wallenstein") was to be performed. The performance was a triumph for Schiller. No care or expense was spared in putting the play on the stage. The costumes were splendid. To the actress (Jagemann) who played Thekla, a lady of Weimar lent a dress which cost twelve thousand *thaler* (nine thousand dollars).

About this time she had occasion to defend Wieland, who was sneered at for retiring to the

country, near Weimar. "The other men of
letters," said Charlotte, "regard him with a
kind of compassion, because he has grown
more patient and indulgent than formerly, and
they ascribe it to the poverty of his spirit, and
his rustic life ; but to me he seems now first
worthy of full respect, because he lives in his
family like a patriarch, and his sons and daughters and grandchildren till the land with him,
and he shows that he has other virtues besides
the literary." Having taken supper with Schiller and Jean Paul Richter at Wolzogen's, where
the talk was very lively, she makes on Richter
this comment : " He is without any pretension,
and in ordinary conversation says admirable
things, but now and then comes a caricaturing
mimicry which has an ungracious air, and
seems even wicked. And this is found in his
writings, intermingled with the sublimest ideas,
which I always like to read over again."

One day Schiller and Goethe dined with her,
and that her feeling towards Goethe is softened
is proved by the following extract from a note
to Lottchen after she and Schiller had returned
to Jena : "August is with me ; his little face
does me good. He wanted to write to your
little Carl, and was delighted with the envelope
I made for him. It is odd that he should have

picked out of my writing-desk the seal, *All for love*, which his father gave me twenty years ago. Don't let Goethe see it." In the autumn she had the joy of meeting Fritz in Leipzig, whither they had both traveled for this purpose, she from Weimar, he from Breslau. A great grief it was to Charlotte to be separated from her favorite son, to whom she had written shortly before, "Thou art the only poetry of my life." Schiller and Lottchen having moved to Weimar, where Goethe had taken a house for them, they celebrated at Christmas with Charlotte her fifty-eighth birthday.

For Weimar a prosperous year was this, the last of the century. Goethe's beautiful poem, "Herman and Dorothea," one of the masterpieces of all literature, had just been published, and Schiller's greatest drama was brought out on the Weimar stage. During the summer of this year might have been seen in the streets of the little capital on the same day, the figures of Wieland, of Goethe, of Herder, of Schiller, of Richter, the five brightest names of German literature, names still kept fresh in the mind of the present generation, in Germany and out of Germany, through the life imparted to work by superior genius.

XVII.

WITH no more apprehensive outlook into the future than on ordinary winter days, Weimar awoke on the first morning of the new century : in the night she had had no dream of the fearful visitation that was to come upon her ere a decade of it had passed over her head. Since the establishment of the Directory in 1795, and the peace between France and Prussia, the alarm caused by the French Revolution had greatly subsided. Bonaparte, after quelling the turbulence of Paris, and then flashing upon the Austrians in Italy, routing them in battle after battle, and making them sign the treaty of Campo Formio, had, in 1798, betaken him to Egypt, to learn in the school of the East lessons in absolutism, lessons for which he had a peculiar aptitude, and which he quickly applied with overpowering force on his return to Paris in the last months of the expiring century. But he had not yet become a terror to Europe. The ambitious, unscrupulous Bonaparte had

not yet hardened into the godless, all-devour-
ing Napoleon.

To the intellectual circle at Weimar the war
in the south made the newspapers lively. The
battle of Marengo, which prostrated Austria,
was too far off that its cannonade should be
heard in the forest of Thuringia as a prelude
to the battle of Jena, which was to prostrate
Prussia. The cultivated Weimar inmates enjoyed as much as ever their plays and other
entertainments. Charlotte was fond of company, of good company, and took part in the
round of meetings and parties, social and
æsthetical, and the readings, sometimes, of
French plays, the company distributing the
parts among them. Every Sunday were the
regular court dinners and evening assemblages.
On the birthday of the duchess, Goethe's translation of Voltaire's " Mahomet " was performed
at the theater. Kotzebue gave a grand ball
early in the winter.

Charlotte, however, suffered from headaches,
and her letters to Fritz complained of the de-
struction to all inward feeling by so much dis-
sipation. She was often sad with a longing to
be with Fritz. Her niece, Amelia Imhoff, attracted a rich lover in a young Swiss physician, who was first to go on his travels, and

she was to give him her hand at the end of
two years. Charlotte thought Amelia "had
more feeling in her imagination than in her
heart, and that made her a poetess." She believed the same of Goethe and Schiller, that
the heart had little to do with their work. In
this opinion as to the substance of poetry she
was all wrong psychologically. No poetry sur-
vives that does not come out of inward depths
of feeling, and this is why one hears no more
of what her niece composed, and why generally
so much verse lives but for a generation, and
some, that is at first popular, hardly so long.

Lottchen writes to Fritz: "The living so
near your dear mother is to me a happiness
which I sometimes fear I only dream ; we pass
many hours together, and when I don't see her
often I long for her. Goethe and Mayer, who
visit Schiller frequently, and take a cordial
interest in us, are still the principal figures in
our family circle here." Charlotte describes to
Fritz one of her parties : "Yesterday the reading club was with me. I fortified the company
with syllabub, which they much relished, and
with galabread and flat cakes, which the cross
Marie and the grumbling Schach had made
very good. "Zaïre" was read. Papa Haren was
overjoyed to play Orosman, the lover of Fräu-

lein von Wolfskeel, who was Zaïre. The Parody was also read; in that he was still better. Your little aunt read the part of Lusignan. She asked me to lay my hand on her heart to feel how the reading of that part made her heart beat. Too lazy to rise from my chair, I said, 'I know very well thy little heart beats very easily;' and there burst forth such a universal laugh that I began to pity her. She turned to me and said I was malicious, and she should not soon forget it." The "little aunt" had shown a tenderness for Camille Jourdan who had been residing for some time in Weimar, and whose recent departure had been a grief to her.

Charlotte was never dazzled by the glare of Bonaparte's success. While the most of those around her were admiring him as the warrior-hero of astounding deeds, and as the man who had subdued the revolution, to her he was hateful for his greed of conquest. Herein she showed that she had a clearer insight into him than Goethe had.

Amelia Imhoff continued to be a source of dissatisfaction to her: "In Wilhelmsthal she has written some pretty poems, but she is so in love with herself, that it is disgusting, and makes her ridiculous; she has not the slightest tact about what should be said and what should not, and because she is now more in the world, it strikes one the more. The duchess complains to me constantly of her [she was maid of honor] ; I tell her of it over and over, but she does not change ; literary geniuses are an absurd race."

With Lottchen Charlotte celebrated the last day of the year by staying till past midnight at a general club-ball, for which Goethe had arranged the opening procession of maskers. He and Schiller were both in fine spirits, but after midnight they withdrew into an adjoining room with two philosophers, Schelling and Steffens, at which the ladies were in great indignation.   There was an "aristocratic" quartette !   Can we be sure that the midnight talk in that "adjoining room" was sparkling or profound ?

A dangerous illness that Goethe had in the beginning of 1801 revealed to Charlotte how dear he still was to her.   For some time his life was despaired of.   "The Schillers and I," she writes to Fritz, "have in the last few days shed many tears over him."   Goethe recovered rapidly.   He wrote her a note of thanks for the sympathy she had shown him.   The duke, setting out for Berlin, came to take leave of him.   The Dowager Duchess Amalia, with her court-ladies, called to congratulate him on his recovery. Charlotte and Lottchen went together to see him. "He begged us for our friendship, as if he were newly arrived in the world. For five days he knew nothing of what was passing. The returning consciousness of himself brought with it, he said, an uncomfortable feeling. He seemed cheerful, but irritable, and broke out angrily because a certain piece of Kotzebue's, "The Desire to Shine," had been given at the theater." Goethe disliked Kotzebue and his plays. A month after Goethe's recovery Lottchen wrote to Fritz: "I love Goethe so cordially, that I can scarcely think of the world without him. Although I see less of him here than in Jena, I nevertheless live with his mind through Schiller, who is almost daily with him. That we women cannot and wish not to have entry into his house *sans façon* is owing to his domestic relations. Although Schiller never sees the lady of the house as companion, and that she never appears at table, yet other people could not believe that she keeps in the background when one of us takes part in the company. You know very well how the people are here, how they watch, and so forth. One would not be safe against a thousand inventions."

The first months of 1802 were lively. Goethe drew upon himself the comments of the large circle of his lady friends, by appearing among the sleigh drivers with Christiane by his side, and she, Christiane, in a silk cloak. One might infer from this, that silk cloaks were not common in sleighs, and that Christiane aimed hereby to overtop the habitual style of sleighing costume, except that poor Christiane does not seem ever to have sought to make herself conspicuous. For the birthday of the duchess Goethe wrote a poetical mask in which his little August played the part of a winged *Amor*, carried about in triumph, and whose duty it was to hand to the duchess the beautiful stanzas Goethe had written. Charlotte is astonished that the duchess, the ideal of dignity and propriety, had not taken exception to "a child of Love" (to use Charlotte's own expression) coming before her as Amor. Possibly, the duchess, a woman of great common sense, with no prudery or nonsense about her, and who had not, like Charlotte, a personal cause for disliking the way in which this particular representative of Amor had come into the world, deemed, on the contrary, that August was just the boy to play the god of Love, a god who, in ancient days, had no respect for

human rites and conventionalities, and who
seems not entirely to have changed his nature
in modern days. Especially troubled was Charlotte on account of the Russian ladies present.
Probably these ladies, accustomed to a large
city, and to a much larger circle than that of
Weimar, took less offensive note of the Au-
gustan Amor than Charlotte herself. What
quiet enjoyment, heightened by his sense of
humor, Goethe, the philosopher, poet, father,
must have had in thus publicly introducing his
beautiful boy to the high exclusive society of
Weimar.

Then came the failure and the fun of Kotzebue's attempt to get up a grand festival in the
state-house in honor of Schiller on the fifth of
March, his birthday, when his bust was to be
formally crowned. Preparations on an impos-
ing scale were made, poems already written,
when the whole fell through, from the impos-
sibility of getting the use of the bust of Schiller, which happened to be in a department
under Goethe's control. Schiller took little
interest in the affair; and as it was gotten up
by Kotzebue to give a blow to Goethe, there
seems to have been a poetical justice in the
scheme's being defeated by him whom it was
designed to injure. The absurd issue of the
undertaking greatly amused Charlotte.

The duchess and several other of her friends were absent for a part of the summer, and she describes herself: "I shall now enjoy solitude under my orange-trees, and again draw, if my eyes will let me, read, and write, as it silently brings me in money, which I apply to good works." She had written two or three comedies, which, perhaps, Schiller's influence had got introduced on one or other of the German theaters. Probably she wrote for the annuals and other periodical publications. Strange as it may seem, a negotiation was opened with Cotta to get "Dido" published, but happily that came to naught.

This summer died, aged over eighty years, the mother of Charlotte, Frau von Schardt, the patient wife and dutiful parent. The loss of even so aged a mother made for a time a void in the affectionate heart of Charlotte. Soon after she had a mortification in the failure of a match she had planned for Fritz, and which fell through owing to some precipitancy of his. Fritz seemed to be saddened by his grandmother's death, and Lottchen, referring to this, he answered her: "I am not unhappy, but, on the contrary, happy and often joyful. So long as I can, I will be industrious and active, and I shall always be glad to remember that I have known the most distinguished people of the age, that I had the truest, warmest friends, that I possessed the best mother and grandmother, that I have enjoyed what is pure, beautiful, and high, that I have not abused my power, and that I never bowed myself unbecomingly to higher power." In the early part of the next year she had a great fright about Fritz. Not having heard from him for an unusually long time, she one day received a letter in a strange hand. Fritz was doing well, but had been wounded in the right arm in a duel.

Meanwhile Schiller had brought out his "Bride of Messina," and Goethe was writing his "Natural Daughter." The death of Klopstock drew from Charlotte this exclamation, "Now all our pious poets are gone, — Gleim, Klopstock, Lavater." Of the poetry of this worthy trio might be said what was said of a more modern poet in another language, " poor, but pious."

At last Charlotte paid her visit to Fritz, reading Goethe's " Faust " and Rousseau's " Confessions " on the ten days' journey to Breslau, near to which Fritz had bought an estate and castle, " not of so mediæval, knightly an air as Kochberg." Fritz had just missed another promising matrimonial chance, simply by the performance on the Breslau stage of " The Cru-

saders," a piece which threw some ridicule
·upon the Roman priesthood. Fritz stood very
well with Countess Haugwitz, who was rich
and pretty, when her father, an out and out
Catholic, and wrathful at this performance,
declared she should never marry a Lutheran.

After a long and happy visit to Fritz, Charlotte returned to Weimar in June, 1803. Her
friends hastened delighted to see her, among
them the duke, who carried off with him a
bottle of some superfine *liqueur* she had
brought, after he had taken a taste of it. Amelia Imhoff had just resigned her post as maid
of honor, and shortly afterwards married her
Swiss lover Helvig. In the middle of July
Charlotte writes to Fritz: "Thou art well, I
hope; for it is calm in my soul, and thou art
part of it." That the wound inflicted by
Goethe's "desertion" was not yet entirely
healed is evident from her charging him with
want of heart because, when she and the
Helvigs were taking tea with the Schillers,
Goethe came in, but after a little time took
Schiller off into another room, where, over a
bottle of wine, they had a long talk and did
not return to the company. The fact was that
Goethe had come to see Schiller on important
business, in regard to which he sought Schiller's aid.

Always having the desire, not unaccompanied by fear, that Fritz should find a mate, in October she heard with joy that he was betrothed to the very young daughter of Baron von Stosch, the wedding, however, not to take place until the next May.

In Weimar the current of life flowed in its wonted way, sometimes quickened by fresh incidents, now and then turned into an eddy by death. Schiller had adapted a play, "The Parasites," to the stage. The master of the forests, with all the lovers of the chase, celebrated St. Hubert's Day on the third of November; and a jovial affair it was, at which, nevertheless, were present Schiller and Knebel. Charlotte herself gave a large tea-party. On Lottchen's birthday she took tea with her and could talk of her anxieties about Fritz, whose urgent request to have the wedding earlier than May, might, she feared, offend the parents of his betrothed, who was only sixteen. She thus concludes a letter to Fritz: " I fear thou hast my fate: few of my wishes and hopes have been fulfilled, although they were very moderate: the last aim of my wishes was, to live with thee, and I thought I had sacrificed that to thy better fortune, and therefore the more am I distressed at thy want of good

fortune. My representations will seem to thee
very hypochondriacal : but for all that, for every
thinking man I see a morning redness that is
never overclouded, namely, a purpose ever to
become better, and that must lead to something better."

The exciting event of this winter was the
arrival, on the fourteenth of December, of
Madame de Staël. On the fifteenth Charlotte
dined with her at the palace, and the next day
sent this sketch to Fritz : " Madame de Staël
is plump, but her mind is so active that she
seems to know nothing of any of her bodily
movements ; she speaks astonishingly fast and
expresses herself beautifully. She got into a
dispute with Schiller about the Kantian philosophy ; but, unhappily, Schiller is not master
enough of French to convert her. To hear a
dispute about the Kantian philosophy in the
rooms of state, in presence of the formal court-
circle, was quite comical to me. Early this
forenoon Wieland and Schiller visited her."

Above the stir and mental movement caused
by the coming of Madame de Staël, was hovering
the serene, benignant Angel of Death. Charlotte writes of Herder's going through severe
bodily suffering, " ere he can pass over into
the long beneficent sleep ; " as though death,

instead of being a sleep, were not a waking as out of a dream. She adds : "Death has to me nothing disagreeable but the place where one is laid. Could I remain lying in my little cabinet, there would be to me nothing forbidding in the thought of death." Such is the lack of spirituality in the prevalent religious feeling and conception, that in looking into a grave the mourners have no clear conviction but that their departed friend is really about to be buried there. Many who call themselves Christians, without feeling or appreciating the spiritual essence of Christ's teaching and example, might learn a lesson from the pagan Socrates, who bore about with him an absolute, paramount consciousness that he was a spirit, and that the earth-treading bodily Socrates was only a temporary shadow of the real Socrates. To the friends who, in his last hour, told him they would see to his being becomingly buried, he answered, " You will have to catch me first."

On the seventeenth of December Charlotte's sister Imhoff died suddenly, and on the same day came news of the death, in the West Indies, of Ernest Imhoff, a young, handsome, promising son of her sister. On the eighteenth, Herder was released from his earthly trials, and passed into a world where is known no pain or poverty but that of the spirit.

When Madame de Staël arrived Goethe was in Jena, and although an express was sent after him by the duke, he did not return to Weimar until the twenty-fourth, for which day, through Lottchen, he invited Madame de Staël to dine with him, with no other company but Schiller and Lottchen.

The Christmas and birthday of Charlotte were this year very sad.

On the eighteenth of January, 1804, Charlotte wrote once more to Fritz about Madame de Staël, whom she had met again at court : " She is liked by everybody, by great and small, young and old, learned and unlearned. With all her intellect she has something very good-natured, seems to be frank, and has the expression of her thoughts through words at her command in a degree that I never knew in any other person. Thou wouldst fall in love with her. Her countenance, too, is agreeable to me, and the more you look at her the better you like her. The duke takes greatly to her and she seems to like him the best of all our gentlemen."

On the first of March Madame de Staël left Weimar. "Goethe," writes Charlotte to Fritz, "was so rejoiced at her departure, that two days in succession he drove through all the streets in a sleigh with his more suitable donna." Like a black drop thrown into a vase of clearest water, the mention of Christiane muddled the transparency of Charlotte's mind and obscured her judgment; but the sight of Christiane by Goethe's side seemed to poison her very being. Instead of the true mirror that she ordinarily was, she became perverted into a distorting reflector which made poor Goethe look hideous. And so she adds: "I am surprised he has not answered the announcement of thy coming marriage: if he has no heart, he should at any rate have good breeding."

What she said of Goethe's joy at getting rid of Madame de Staël was true. Both Schiller and Goethe were somewhat bored by her. Neither of them enjoyed such torrents of talk. After she had been in Weimar several weeks, Schiller writes to Goethe: "She will learn from personal experience that we Germans are a changeable people, and that visitors ought to know when it is time to go." Schiller was sailing prosperously on the breezy current of poetic creation, hard at work on "William Tell;" to be obliged to heave to and go ashore for any purpose was a misery. He writes to

Goethe : " I am now near the end of my work, and must carefully guard against whatever might disturb or rob me of the indispensable last mood, but especially against all French friends." To Schiller Goethe wrote : " Our distinguished traveler. told me to-day, with the greatest *naïveté,* that she should print every word that I uttered, in so far as she could get hold of them." That was quite enough to tether Goethe's tongue. After Schiller's first talk with Madame de Staël at the palace, he drew an unprejudiced, discriminating sketch of her in a letter to Goethe, in which he says : " For what we call poetry she has no sense ; in such works she can only prize what is passionate, rhetorical, or general."

Notwithstanding that ebullition against Goethe, Charlotte's relation with him continued to grow more friendly. Goethe gave her a standing invitation to his Thursday morning receptions, where the company, chiefly ladies, conversed and looked at engravings, etc : " I always take a lady with me, and learn all kinds of things, for one should keep learning. I stay from eleven till one." Yet, she cannot withhold a hit, for she concludes: " I believe Madame de Staël has produced in him the *besoin* of consorting again with more cultivated women than he for some time has had about him."

Then came the journey of Schiller and Lott-chen to Berlin, where Schiller was received with universal enthusiasm, saw his plays per-formed with brilliant success, was honored by the king, who made him proposals to establish himself in Berlin, proposals which, had they been more liberal, would probably have been accepted, the effect of which was to induce the open-handed Karl August, whose means were comparatively limited, to make him a larger allowance.

Laharpe, the French author and critic, and tutor of the Emperor Alexander, passed through Weimar and gave Goethe an alarming picture of the power and ambition of Napoleon, which threatened to subjugate the world. "But no tyrant," said Goethe, "can subdue the power of human reason;" a judgment as noble as it is profound.

A momentous event for Weimar was the marriage of the crown-prince to a Russian princess, Maria Paulowna. Great was the jubi-lation and lively the festivities, on the arrival of the newly-married pair in November, 1804. For the reception of the princess Schiller wrote his "Homage of the Arts." At the theater in the course of the week, were per-formed Schiller's "William Tell," Goethe's

16

"Sisters," and his remodeled "Goetz von Berlichingen." To Karl August it was a proud
reflection that no regal or imperial sovereign
through all Europe could give so glorious and
glorifying a greeting to a newly-arrived imperial daughter-in-law as the sovereign of the
dukedom of Weimar. And this he was enabled to do through the elevation and insight
of his own mind, which prompted him to give a
home in his quiet little capital, first to Goethe,
and then to Schiller, and there to honor and
cherish them both.

XVIII.

On the first of January, 1805, Goethe went to see Charlotte. He could not withhold from her the foreboding, that during this year he or Schiller would die. Writing a note to Schiller in the morning, to wish him a happy new year, from his pen came the words, *the last new year*. Affrighted, he tore the paper into fragments. The pen had been for a moment guided by an invisible hand. There had been a mysterious intimation from the deep of futurity, a confidential anticipatory impartance of divine decree, a whisper from the infinite soul to the individual soul, angelic ministration revealing a secret from the dark unknown, causing a wholesome awe, as if one stood for an instant in the unspeakable Presence.

Charlotte began the year with headache. She was, however, able to attend Goethe's Thursday reception on the third. On the ninth he wrote to her hoping she would not fail on the morrow, as the grand-princess was

to be there. Lottchen, too, had an especial invitation. He read to the company something
that particularly pleased them. In a note of
the fourteenth, Schiller tells him: " The grand-
princess spoke of the interest she took in what
you read. She enjoys what she sees and hears
at your house." To which Goethe answers: " If
our young princess finds enjoyment in what
we are able to impart to her, our wishes are
fully satisfied. One of us can only say with
the apostle, — Silver and gold have I none,
but what I have that I give unto you in the
name of the Lord."

In February Goethe had so dangerous an illness (lung fever) that Charlotte wrote to Fritz:
"Goethe has just sent August to me to say
that Stark has pronounced him out of danger.
Poor Einsidel, too, has been many months ill,
also of an affection of the lungs. Princess Caroline (daughter of Karl August and Louise)
has likewise been suffering with an abscess in
the ear for more than four weeks. For some
time past she was quite dispirited. So young
and so afflicted! It often seems to me as
though it were not worth while to come into
the world. But Solomon said that long ago."
Schiller, too, was ill in February, and was not
able to leave the house before the beginning of

March. He then went to Goethe. They had not seen each other for several weeks. Both were affected to tears as they embraced.

In the friendship between Goethe and Schiller there is a nobleness that is rare and instructive. It was a friendship sanctified by the spirit of Damon and Pythias. The high plane on which their lives moved, together with the brilliant and honorable success of both, put a seal of finer beauty to the bond that united them. That bond, kept warm by reciprocal affection and admiration, was never chilled by envy or jealousy or misunderstanding. Between them was a mutuality of highest services, the frank interchange of philosophic and poetic thought, a community, not of worldly goods, but of what is more precious, of spiritual and intellectual goods. One of Goethe's good fortunes was his intimacy with Schiller. This was to him as profitable, in a different way, as his intimacy with Charlotte von Stein. Each intimacy lasted ten years, and each was only possible to a man of large emotions, of aspiring aims, of sound character. The good fortune of Goethe was blooming and fruitful, because in his individuality fortune found so rich a soil. He had the means and the will to make the most of good opportunities. A barren-minded man may have a stroke or two of luck, but it will not be prolific or continuous. Napoleon's "star" owed its rise and culmination and its brilliancy to his intellectual calibre and military genius; its setting to his moral sterility. Fortune is subordinate, and no human might is allowed to "circumvent God."

On account of ill health and loneliness Charlotte had for some time desired to have live with her a lady-companion. A suitable one she thought she had found in Caroline von Bose, a friend of the Knebels. Charlotte thus wrote of her to Fritz: "She has a good disposition, appreciates cultivated discourse, and does not live for visiting, cards, and gossip." The lady did not turn out to be entirely deserving of the latter part of this eulogy. In the mean time Charlotte had established with the Princess Caroline and the Grand-Princess Maria Paulowna a very cordial relation and a solid, resting on sympathy and mutual respect. The crown-prince, too, was sociable with her, coming often to her in the evening.

In April, Goethe had another illness: only his nearest friends had access to him. Schiller seemed better than usual; but on the twenty-ninth, while at the theater, he was attacked with fever, which left him the next day weak and exhausted. On the sixth of May he felt so much better after a bath, that he and his friends had fresh hope ; but towards evening his head was seized, and in the night he became delirious. He lingered for two days in a slumbering state, and passed away in the night of the ninth of May, 1805.

. In these the bitterest hours of Lottchen's life Charlotte was at her side. To Goethe the death of Schiller was a heavy blow. He loved Schiller, and they leaned the one upon the other. To Zelter he wrote : " I thought to lose myself, and instead of that, I lose a friend, and in him the half of my being." In his grief he had recourse to Charlotte. " Goethe is entirely recovered," she writes to Fritz ; " he comes oftener to me. Schiller is an irreparable loss to him. To-day he spoke so beautifully of the physical and the intellectual man, that I ought to have written it down." Charlotte was with Lottchen as much as her own headaches would allow her to be. On the afternoon of June first, she accompanied the duchess and the grand-princess to see Lottchen.

To Schiller's widow, for her two boys, the crown-prince gave four hundred *thaler* (about three hundred dollars) yearly, with an addition when they should go to the University. Schiller

left to his family nothing but his works and a
good and great name. Nevertheless, such trib-
ute was paid to his genius, that his wife was
pecuniarily better off after his death than when
he lived. From different parts of Germany
pensions were bestowed which raised her an-
nual income to fifteen hundred *thaler.* Quoting from, I believe, Schiller, Charlotte says :
" A heart has gone before her, and sparkling
binds her to a higher world. Schiller," she
continues, " was buried very privately, but, I
hear, a monument will be erected to him in the
new cemetery, and that his remains will be carried thither. I saw him just after he expired,
and his countenance seemed to me much dis-
figured."

Another man of large original mental power,
one of the small eminent class of great discov-
erers, appeared at Weimar this summer ; and
delivered in the palace — where superior mind
was ever welcomed — a course of lectures on
his vast recent discovery of the physiology of
the brain, lectures attended by the ducal family and the court, and others. This was Gall.
Charlotte was captivated by his exposition.
In a letter to Fritz, a short time afterwards,
she arrests a movement in her to cavil at something Goethe had done, with this reflection :

" When one has heard Gall, one becomes very indulgent to the conduct of people, and discovers that many a virtue deserves no higher place than many a fault. His doctrine does not lead to materialism, but, on the contrary, to something highly spiritual."

For part of the summer and early autumn Goethe was absent. On returning home he began at his house, every Wednesday forenoon, discourses and conversations on natural science, which Charlotte attended regularly. She had good news from Fritz, become the happy father of a daughter. But by the clouds of war all minds were darkened. Twenty thousand Prussian soldiers were quartered upon the Duchy of Weimar. In November the grand-princess had the joy of welcoming, in her new Weimar home, her brother, the Emperor Alexander, on his way to the fatal field of Austerlitz.

Charlotte's Christmas birthday was again a sad one, although she had about her many friends, among them the Princess Caroline, the crown-prince and his consort, the grand-princess, with tears in her " Asiatic " eyes. Describing, in a letter to Fritz, the general anxety, she says : " Must there not be a hell in the breast of the conqueror to whom are sent so many thousands of curses from oppressed humanity ? " Napoleon's hell on earth was reserved for St. Helena ; and even there it was a hell of baffled greed and humbled pride rather than of accusing conscience.

XIX.

·

THE SACK OF WEIMAR.

THE year 1806 opened ominously in Weimar. The streets were filled with wagons, horses, artillery, the air with sounds of warlike preparation, all hearts with forebodings. Karl August was a general in the Prussian service.

On the third of March Charlotte writes to Fritz : " One could again enjoy the all-vivifying spring, if the great murderer were not alive on the earth." She longed to see Fritz and his wife, but she was, she wrote, too ill and old for such a journey. She stayed at home, and the grand-princess sent every day to her door a carriage and horses for her to drive out. Early in the summer Goethe went to Carlsbad. One day the duchess invited herself to breakfast with Charlotte. She was calm, wrote Charlotte to Lottchen, and " remarked, as if upon herself, that one would not grow better, if one expended one's self too much upon society, and that solitude did her good."

In September Goethe betook himself to

Jena; the threatening outlook drove him, early
in October, back to Weimar, where all was
uncertainty and apprehension.   The king of
Prussia (an incompetent king) had been duped:
he did not declare war until the eighth of October, when the legions of Napoleon were
already close upon him.   On the eleventh, the
king, his noble wife, the duke of Brunswick,
and many other princes, were in Weimar.   On
the tenth, while the slow king of Prussia was
entering Weimar, the rapid Napoleon was
defeating part of his army at Saalfeld, only
twenty-five English miles south of Weimar.
Charlotte writes to Fritz on the eleventh of
October: " If Bonaparte's fortune does not desert him I have no confidence in our chief
commanders."   Early on the fourteenth, the
Dowager Duchess Amalia, with the Crown-
Prince and Princess Caroline, fled to Erfurt.

In the forenoon of that day was heard in
Weimar the fearful roar of nearer-sounding
cannon.   In the afternoon, about four o'clock,
was raised the terrible cry, " The French are
coming."   A little later cannon-balls flew over
or struck in the town.   Then came, retreating
from Jena, the routed Prussians, hotly pursued
by the French.   Behind Goethe's house and
by that of Charlotte rushed the flying Prus-

sians. French hussars and dragoons spread quickly through the town. Food and lodging they demanded, and forcibly took what was not given them. The whole night and the next day went on the plundering. In a letter, written to Fritz a week afterwards, Charlotte describes what she had gone through in that dreadful night : " During the terrible cannonade they brought to me a Prussian general severely wounded ; this was Count Schmettau. I concealed his uniform, gave him a shirt of your late father, which happened to be there (his own was all bloody), wrapt him in my flannel bathing-gown, bought in haste a woolen night-cap, and so got him to bed, the poor unfortunate. But what a night was before us ! French cavalry were constantly dashing through my yard. A number of them rushed upon my house : this was in the daytime. They demanded wine, and as my maid could not speak French, I took heart to tell them they must wait for the keys to be brought. They took eight Pyrmont bottles filled with wine. Now came a second troop : one of them wanted to cut me on the head ; fortunately an officer rushed in and cried : " *Vite, vite ! il n'est pas le temps à boire.*" (Quick, quick ! this is no time for drinking.) Now night set in ; the dreadful cannonade ceased. Mother Seebach and Schach, who took care of Schmettau, were still in the house. Not a soul thought of their plundering the town. All at once three Frenchmen force themselves in, demand brandy and bread, and as I had given out all I had, they at last go off. One of them takes my watch, misses his way, I hold him fast between a door, he gives it back to me, but says : "*Fermez votre porte ; il en viendront d'autres, qui vous la prendront.*" (Shut your door ; others will come along who will take it from you.) I fastened my door tight. Then there was a cry of fire. Through the night there was knocking and uproar ; I threw them money out of the window (for victuals and wine I had no more) and many went away. At last there came a great crowd, broke through the front door, and forced Schach to take them to a shop ; they dragged him about an hour and a half before he returned. Four times I sent to Prince Murat for a safeguard for Count Schmettau ; it was promised, but never came. The duchess sent for me twice, but I would not and could not leave poor Schmettau. At last, after midnight, it was more quiet. Without undressing I lay down on the bed, but could not sleep on account of the beating of my heart. As day dawned I got up. All at once they broke into my house from three sides, in the upper story from Countess Henckel, below through the Greek church, and through one of my doors. I went out of my room. On the stair-way I was surrounded by as many as fifty soldiers; they said to me, " *Ouvrez les portes ! ouvrez les armoires !*" (Open the doors ! open the closets !) The first press was soon opened, but swiftly I ran to the state-house and stood before the bed of a sleeping general; his name was Marchand. He got up in haste, and went with me. General Marchand seemed humane, and also another officer. Poor Schmettau was obliged to go on foot with all his wounds to the palace, for the officer said there was no safety in private houses. General Marchand drove the robbers out of the house with blows and thrusts of his sword. He promised me a safeguard in two hours. As Schach had to go with the unfortunate Schmettau to the palace, and I had nobody left, I went along holding the arm of the officer, and did not, like Lot's wife, look behind me. Now they had a free field for plundering." Three days later she went to see Count Schmettau, who had just breath enough left to thank her. He died the next day.

While Charlotte was proving herself a heroine, another woman, under a neighboring roof, was doing the same. Goethe's house was destined for General·Augereau, and some cavalry. The young French hussar officer who rode up to announce this to him was the son of Lili. A number were lodged in the servants' rooms below, and the back building was a refuge for many inhabitants of the town. Late at night two marauders got into the house, called for wine, made the master of the house drink with them, asked for beds, rushed upstairs, got into Goethe's room, tried to seize him, threatened his life. Christiane called to the back building for help and turned them out, showing, through all the trials of the frightful period, presence of mind, courage, judgment, and devotion. In the morning General Augereau arrived, and sentinels guarded the house.

Five days after the battle of Jena, that is, on Sunday, the nineteenth of October, in the city, church, by the city pastor, Günther, Goethe was formally married to Christiane Vulpius. Notwithstanding the deep depression of all classes in Weimar from the ravages and losses and outrages of war, which, one might have thought, would have chastened them, especially the cultivated class, into good feeling and common sense through affliction, this moral, in all respects proper, act caused in " society " another howl, in which, I am grieved to say, was particularly lugubrious and unhuman the note of my dear heroine and that of her friend Lottchen ; and this against an act, in doing which Goethe fulfilled a fourfold duty, a duty towards the state, towards society, towards Christiane, towards himself. In certain stages and conditions of civilization, self-complacent prejudice so chokes the growth of principle, that conventionalities, through the force of custom, clothe themselves almost with the authority of law.

Had praise been offered to Charlotte and Christiane for their doings on that terrible night, with the diffidence of spontaneous virtue they would have answered that they had only done their duty. If we all did our duty always, what a glorious world this would be transformed into! To do their duty in such trials as they were suddenly put to stamps them heroines. Doubtless, in that night, other women of Weimar, in lower stations, for the protection of children · or parents or husbands, did their duty as fully as Charlotte and Christiane. In the very alarms of woman there is a quality which love turns into daring.

17

Within the palace, — which she never had
·a thought of deserting, — was another woman
whose deeds are of the class that ennoble history.   When in the evening Napoleon entered
the ducal palace, which the morning-victory of
Jena made his, at the head of the stair-way
stood a lady, calmly waiting to receive him.
Napoleon started as his eyes fell upon her.
"*Qui êtes vous?*" (Who are you?) he exclaimed.   "I am the duchess of Weimar."   "I
pity you: I shall crush your husband."   He
then added, "I shall dine in my apartment,"
and hastened by her.   But the heart of the
ruthless conqueror was touched.   A few moments afterwards he said to General Rapp:
"There is a woman whom our two hundred
cannon have not been able to make tremble."

Early the next morning the duchess sent her
chamberlain to request an audience of the emperor.   He returned a gracious answer and
invited himself to breakfast with her.   On entering, he said, abruptly: "How could your
husband, madame, be so mad as to make war
upon me?"   "Your majesty would have despised him if he had not."   "How so?" was the
quick reply.   The duchess rejoined with dignity: "My husband has been in the service of
Prussia for more than thirty years, and surely

it was not at the moment when the king had so
mighty an enemy as your majesty to contend
against, that the duke could abandon him."
This admirable answer put Napoleon into a
good mood. The conversation went on so
prosperously for the duchess that at last Napoleon exclaimed: "Madame, you are the most
estimable woman I have ever known; you have
saved your husband." The duchess seized the
happy moment to intercede for her suffering
people. Napoleon gave orders for the plundering to cease.

When, after a few days, Charlotte went back
to her house, she found doors and windows
smashed, all her presses and wardrobes broken
open, everything of any value carried off, and
her papers strewn about the floor. Fifty or
sixty *thaler* were taken out of her writing-
desk. Fortunately, the sum she had laid by
for a journey to Fritz was not discovered. Her
son Karl had to send her a gown to wear. On
the twenty-fourth she wrote to Fritz: "The
mighty fatality that desolates the countries
has also swallowed us up. God protect you
and beautiful Silesia! then I will bear quietly
my afflictions. I have been robbed of everything, like most of the inhabitants of Weimar." After a while were relieved her anxieties

about Fritz, whose estate near Breslau had not
been devastated. Her sixty-fourth birthday
she passed in deep sorrow. On the twenty-
sixth the theater was reopened. The Duchess
Louise, on her entrance, was received with wild
jubilation.

The following sentence, from a letter to
Fritz, is significant of Charlotte's state of mind
at the beginning of the new year. " This world
is a tedious repetition of tyranny, greed, and
lust of conquest, and, what is most laughable,
of pride. Poor human nature! but happily
richly gifted with levity and short-sightedness."
By degrees she grew more composed. She
took to reading again. Goethe sent her new
books. "As from my childhood," she wrote,
" I have been attracted to the starry heavens, I
am interested in the discovery of three new
small planets." In February, the Monday
evening unions were recommenced at her
house, she having to borrow tea-spoons for the
company. On the first of April Goethe resumed his Wednesday meetings. Nine days
later the whole population was thrown into
grief by the death of the Dowager Duchess
Amalia, the benefactress of the duchy, the
early friend of Charlotte, who entered adult life
as her maid of honor more than forty years be-

fore. Amalia died of a broken heart, of grief at the oppression and misery of her beloved Duchy of Weimar.

But things social began to run in their old channels. On the first of May Charlotte took tea with the duchess in company with Wieland and Goethe. Just after that she had the joy of welcoming under her roof her son Fritz, with his wife and two children. Goethe made his usual visit to Carlsbad, whence he wrote to Charlotte, but through the hand of a secretary, a reminder to her of their changed relation to each other; but his letters grew more frequent, and their meetings were more kindly.

Then came, in the early autumn of 1808, the assemblage of emperors and kings at Erfurt, where chains of fascination were still more closely thrown by the strong Napoleon over the comparatively weak Alexander, who at Tilsit had recently been cajoled by the plausibilities and magnetized by the genius of his upstart brother-emperor. The delusion of Alexander in regard to Napoleon, unshaken by the subjugation and prostration of Germany, was dispelled when the Corsican cormorant, in 1812, clutched, with his bloody talons, at the Russian eagle. Your egoism is a great demolisher as well as weaver of delusions.

In company with Karl August, Goethe went to Erfurt, and had an interview with Napoleon. After two or three days he returned to Weimar, where all the emperors and kings and grandees were to be entertained, and where the "Cæsar" of Voltaire was to be performed at the theater by Napoleon's troupe of French actors. Charlotte writes to Fritz: "We are to see here soon all the Princes, Kings, Emperors of Europe. To-morrow they are expected at a hunt in Ettersburg: there one can see them by paying for tickets. Those who subscribe first, get the best places. I am too good an economist (particularly as this very day I had to pay again for taxes ten *thaler* and five *groschen*) to give out money for what would give me no enjoyment ; for I am so simple as to pity the poor stags that are chased out of their forests more than the kings that are driven out of their kingdoms."

The imperialities and royalties lodged in the palaces, their attendant ministers and generals with the chief residents of the town. Charlotte, in the same letter to Fritz, says, " I don't know who is to lodge with me. Talleyrand is my neighbor in the apartment of Countess Henckel." An amusing incident shows how the Weimar gentlemen had to bestir themselves for the regal guests. Goethe came in one morning to Charlotte's, and after a few words fell fast asleep. On being accidentally awakened by the entrance of another lady, he apologized on account of unusual fatigue and exhaustion, and then involuntarily went off to sleep again.

But this was a short carnival, gotten up to feed the vanity and strengthen the power of the insatiate despot, the inflated semi-barbarian, the imperial *parvenu*, the necessary scourge of degenerate legitimacy, himself an impossible permanent sovereign in the nineteenth century. Ghastly festivities were these, like a wedding on a battle-field during a pause in the carnage. Following this carnival was a long lent, of several years, for Weimar, for Germany, a universal deprivation, a general degradation and despair. The Emperor Alexander, after dancing at the palace-ball until five o'clock in the morning, took leave of his new Titanic friend, who hastened westward, to organize more bloodshed, and still astound Europe with his Asiatic career.

In Weimar the current of human life flowed on again with its wonted movement, seemingly the slower for this momentary tempestuous interruption. The presence of superior mind gives at all times quiet animation to a community. Herder and Schiller were gone, and Amalia, but Wieland and Goethe were left, and Karl August with his high consort, Louise, and others who were in close sympathy with these, foremost among them Charlotte von Stein. Marriages and deaths made the usual ripples in the social stream. Wolzogen, Lott-chen's brother-in-law, passed away. Herder's wife ascended to where her husband was enjoying a higher existence. Charlotte was always ready for a good new book. About this time Alfieri's Autobiography appeared, with which her independent spirit could warmly sympathize. Every now and then they had a foretaste of Goethe's best. He read to them the first part of " The Elective Affinities," admiration of which made them eager for the remainder. Here was, indeed, a *new* book. An interesting event, but a sad one to Charlotte, on account of parting with a dear friend, was the marriage of the Princess Caroline to the crown-prince of Mecklenburg. Between the princess and Charlotte had grown up a warm friendship, the warmth, in this case, heightened by difference of age.

To early associates and friends Charlotte found herself drawn closer, to the Knebels, to

·the duchess, to Goethe. Her intimacy with the grand-princess continued. With Lottchen the ties of a maternal tenderness, woven twenty years before, had never been loosened. But she was kept anxious by the pecuniary affairs of her two sons, whose estates were burdened with new taxes and old debts. Fritz continued to reside in Silesia. Weimar, having been joined to the Confederation of the Rhine, had to furnish its contingent to the armies of Napoleon, to march whithersoever he ordered them. In 1810 Charlotte writes: "Most of our officers in Spain have been killed, — Colonel Egloffstein, Staff, and another whose name I don't know ; also Gray. And ever must more be led out to be slaughtered. I would rather slay my grandsons myself than so give them up."

Through tribulation, through humiliation, through every kind of suffering, rolled the dreary days and weeks and months and years in Germany into 1812, when Charlotte entered her seventieth year. On the fifteenth of December she had the joy of learning that on that day Napoleon rushed through Weimar in a sleigh, fleeing from the wrath behind him, his brow black with forebodings of the wrath to come.

XX.

In the beginning of 1813 Weimar was beset with as deep anxieties and as menacing troubles as just before the battle of Jena in 1806. Poor Weimar was between two fires. To save his people from worse, Karl August had felt it to be his hard duty to join the *Confederation of the Rhine.* Detesting and groaning under French rule, Weimar might, nevertheless, as being thus an ally of Napoleon, be treated as an enemy by the Russians. The king of Prussia having just declared war against France, she was so treated by a detachment of Prussian cavalry, who took prisoners the Weimar contingent, much, probably to the satisfaction of the contingent.

So excited and unhappy was Goethe at the state of public affairs, that his wife insisted on his setting out for Toeplitz, whither the grand-princess had already gone. "Misery makes us acquainted with strange bedfellows." Christiane, who had never before set foot in Char-

lotte's house, came, the day after his departure,
to announce it to her ; and Charlotte, in writing of the visit, makes no ungracious comment.
In April, the French, coming in force, drove
out the Prussians. Napoleon, for the moment,
had his head-quarters at Erfurt. He was in
Weimar part of a day and treated the duchess
with great respect. Of Louise, Lottchen
writes on the first of May : " The duchess is,
indeed, an extraordinary woman, always up to
the level of great events, always calm and
clear ; her countenance and bearing do me
good."

In the middle of May Charlotte writes to
Fritz : " One cannot write much ; one must
suffer and keep silent. I am worn out by the
everlasting tumult and beating of drums. For
twelve nights I have not fairly gone to bed. I
wonder how at seventy one can bear so many
anxieties and sorrows." In a letter to Lottchen,
speaking of a particularly hard case, she adds :
" Many a one is especially persecuted by fate :
and now there comes into the world a man who
outbids fate." To Fritz she wrote : " Oh, if I
could hear no more drumming and ringing of
soldiers to quarters. Many people die because
rest is no more to be had." Commenting to
Lottchen on the crown-prince, who, she fears

will not be able to retain the love of his wife,
she says : " How few men know how to treat
a tender womanly heart, — and he least of all."
Out of the high Weimar circle Death, in his
customary rounds, carried off two members, —
the sprightly Wieland, in his eightieth year, and
the genial sister of Knebel.

Amid the marchings, the tramplings of cavalry, the roll of drums, and all the restlessness
of instant war, here is an idyllic episode, which
comes upon us with a humorous surprise.   For
Goethe's birthday, the twenty-eighth of August,
Charlotte, as she had done years before with
the Princess Caroline, had a large pine-apple
ready to present to him.   As Goethe did not
return to Weimar until September, one moon-
light evening Charlotte with her maid went
through her garden into his ; but perceiving
that near him was seated the actress Engels,
one of his favorites from the theater, who was
singing to him with a guitar, she silently
pushed the pine-apple on the ground towards
him and retired, having received, says Duentzer, "a thrust in the heart, from seeing him in
such unworthy company."

Now came the great battle of Leipzig, which
liberated Germany, but the first effects of which
were disastrous to the inhabitants of Weimar,

trampled on and pillaged by the flying French, and not less by the pursuing Cossacks. By heroic uprising, Germany had shaken off the French yoke ; by great deeds of arms and noble sacrifices, had regained her high position. Charlotte's strong German feeling could now swell within her breast unarrested by thoughts of Napoleonic dominion, uncompressed by any sense of humiliation. Her seventy-second birthday she celebrated in comparative calmness and enjoyment.

But soon the mighty lion was at large again. He had broken out of his Elban cage and was again spreading consternation over Europe. Neither Charlotte nor Goethe attained to a sound judgment on Napoleon. Few people did in that day. Goethe had too much admiration of the man and his power, Charlotte too much fear. At this time Charlotte was suffering more than usual from gout in the head and eyes. She was, however, denying herself in order to help dear Fritz. Her illustrious friend, Duchess Louise, was doing the same to help her people. Of her, Charlotte writes to Lottchen : "What the duchess is doing for the relief of the land does not surprise me ; she is one of the few princesses capable of every sacrifice." The battle of Waterloo and the second entrance of the allies into Paris took a load from the spirits of Charlotte, and seemed to give her new strength. On her birthday Goethe sent her preserves accompanied by verses written in the old affectionate tone with the cordial *du*.

As Charlotte approached four-score, infirmities grew upon her, and restricted her usefulness as well as enjoyment. She now the more needed attention and kindness from friends; and she was not one whom friends were likely to fail. That which drew them to her, a sprightly, clear intellect and sound judgment, made the sounder by the insight of a sympathetic nature, held old friends fast and earned for her fresh ones. The new generation was attracted to her. Karl's children were devoted to their grandmother, delighting to make her a visit or to have her at Kochberg. Foremost among her earlier associates was the widow of Schiller, dear Lottchen, whom she had loved since Lottchen's childhood. Charlotte's eyes were so affected occasionally that she could neither read nor write. At such times Lottchen would read to her. They had together the privilege of hearing Goethe read from his "Divan," a volume which may be called the poetical residuum of the long life of one who was at once a meditative sage and an active practical man of the world.

Between Goethe and Charlotte were reëstablished intimate relations. In 1816 an event occurred which made these still more close. This was the death of Christiane. Poor Christiane, subjected through life to the exaggerations of gossip and the calumnious comments of malevolence, was pursued by these to her death-bed. And this solely because she was part of Goethe; for Goethe, like all men who rise much above the level of their fellows, was a target at which envy and jealousy aimed their sharpest arrows, whose points were sometimes envenomed with the poison of falsehood. Charlotte, who before Christiane's decease had outlived the worst of her feeling towards her, and who knew so well the affectionateness of Goethe's nature, knew that his grief for the loss of Christiane was real. While giving him her sympathy she could not but feel — and the feeling could not but have in it a secret satisfaction — that a barrier between her and Goethe was removed, and that, although the old attraction could not overleap the quarter of a century elapsed since its breach, to reunite the aged pair in its earlier bond, their friendship would now have freer play, and the concord of their minds on many subjects enjoy warmer personal manifestation.

During this year appeared in Weimar another Charlotte of Goethe's, the Charlotte of Wetzlar and Werther, now the widow Kestner with nine children. She was on a visit to one of her daughters, married in Weimar. What a meeting — if they did meet — between these two immortal Charlottes! In the autumn was published Goethe's " Italian Journey," made up chiefly out of his letters to Charlotte von Stein.

The following year Goethe's son, in whom from his childhood Charlotte had always taken an interest, was married to Ottilie von Pogwish, a sprightly, intelligent lady, and of a pliable nature, who, from the day of her entrance into Goethe's house until his death, proved to be a comfort and a stay, and a good daughter to him in his latter days. Just before the marriage Goethe gave her this wise counsel : " See here, Ottilie, there is one thing I wish to say to thee. My son likes to be praised ; so, you must not contradict him. When you feel inclined to dispute, come to me ; dispute with me, I can bear it."

And thus the unresting years bore Charlotte forward beyond the bound of the usual stretch of human life. Except Knebel, who

reached his ninetieth year, she was the longest-
lived of a long-lived circle. Wieland was eighty
when he passed from the earth to a higher existence; Goethe eighty-three; Karl August,
over seventy; his consort Louise, nearly eighty,
Herder, not quite seventy; Schiller was the
only one who died in middle life, at the age of
forty-six. Length of years, in persons of such
high usefulness, is a blessing to their fellows.
In the richly-endowed, whose faculties have
been well cultivated, and who attain to a high
age, the fuller accomplishment of life's purposes begets a bloom of wisdom which perfumes
a neighborhood. From them radiates creative
warmth upon those who have the susceptibility
and the elevated curiosity to profit by such
presences.

In that fine part of wisdom contributed by
hope, Charlotte was a little deficient. To her
pictures and imaginations of human events and
possibilities a tinge of melancholy gave at times
too dark a shadow. Her religious feeling of
reliance upon overruling spiritual power was
not enough cheered by the hopefulness which
is the happy element in faith, and which, in the
most privileged souls, is ever welling up to an-
ticipate the final consummations of divine supremacy. Her view of life was not enlightened

18

by that kind of inward illumination which vol-
atilizes the grosser parts of human suffering
and calamity, so that they lose the worst of
their weight and obstructiveness. She took
life a little too hardly. She did not hate life,
as the Countess of Albany did after the death
of Alfieri ; nor did she, to the same degree that
the countess did, — and many other people apparently do, — mistake a part of life, the earthly
part, for the whole. There are those who af-
firm that our breathing here is all our being ;
that when the body dies, the man dies ; that for
us there is no continuance, no hereafter ; that
instead of the inheritance of a better life, we
are to have, when we shall have " shuffled off
this mortal coil," the nothingness of absolute
death. Some say they believe this ; but do
they, can they, constituted as the human mind
is, absolutely and finally believe it ? In the
gloomiest folds of such belief there must
twinkle at times a heavenly spark of doubt.
There is no deeper law than that of progres-
sion, of improvement, of aspiration ; and to limit
the range of aspiration to our being and doing
here, were it not to throw a pall over our living
days on earth, as though we were already a
corpse ? Then, as now, such material views
circulated largely, and Charlotte did not entirely escape their contagion.

The fears of Charlotte in regard to her sons had, happily, not been confirmed, and on her eightieth birthday she had the joy of having them both with her, now prosperous gentlemen, esteemed for their intelligent activity, honored for manliness, and both blessed with promising offspring, her grandchildren affectionate and attentive to her. Karl and Fritz, on their part, had the filial satisfaction of seeing their beloved mother, though suffering in body, still lively in mind, still eager for intellectual enjoyment and enlargement, and, through the agency of her own heart and attractiveness, surrounded by devoted friends, the best and highest in her community, chief among them her renowned admirer.

When her eyes would allow it she still held the pen. In February, 1824, she writes to Knebel: " Your letters, dearest friend, are to me poetry without rhyme, and the only thing that still enlivens my life. Through my deafness I am turned entirely inward on myself, and perambulate my past existence, to find if I cannot out of my present experiences get something to improve my future life. There always, however, come *buts* between, which I cannot grasp. Yesterday evening several maskers came to me from the ball. The crown-prince was magnificent. Such scenes strike me now as extraordinary; that the world-spirit has made men invent such buffooneries, while they are at the same time capable of such cruel deeds as I read every day in newspapers and books of travel."

Then came, close upon each other, the three jubilees. First, September third, the fiftieth anniversary of the reign of the Grand-duke Karl August (made grand-duke by the congress of Vienna in 1815), heartily celebrated by all classes of his subjects. The most touching incident of the festival was when Goethe, before the assembled crowd, approached Karl August, and after a silent embrace, delivered to him the medal struck in commemoration of the event. In October was celebrated the golden wedding of Karl August and Louise. And on the seventh of November the fiftieth anniversary of Goethe's arrival in Weimar, a day so especially momentous to Charlotte von Stein. On that day friends and admirers of the great poet flocked into Weimar from far and near.

On the twenty-second of September Charlotte writes to Fritz: "I have neither strength nor recollection enough, dear Fritz, to describe to thee all the festivities of our duke's jubilee;

so much I know, that I missed thee very much, and the grand-duchess was quite troubled that thou wast not there. Also among the crowd of strangers were many of thy acquaintance, who visited me and asked after thee, among others General L'Estocq, who thanked me for the kindness you showed his son in Breslau. The day before yesterday evening I had the whole family of Altensteins to tea with my grandson Karl and his affianced, all excellent people. There were many others; but I sat like a monument — a Shakespearean expression — in my cabinet; for I have nearly lost my speech, can hear no more, and my sight is darkened. Thus wilt thou find me, dear Fritz; and besides, such pains that I cannot walk. Goethe is very kind to me ; if thou canst bring with thee something for him, do so. I fear that my letter will again be too late."

The letter was too late : twenty-four hours after it was dispatched she had the joy of embracing once more her dear Fritz.

For her eighty-fourth birthday she received a letter of congratulation from Lottchen Schiller, then living in Bonn, to which she answered : "Dear Lolo! A thousand thanks for your remembrance on my birthday! May ruling destiny be friendly through life to you all, to Caro-

line and Emily and the good mother. This is
all that my weakness and many pains permit
me to say. Your true Stein." A few weeks
later she was deeply affected by tidings of the
death of this dear friend.

She herself grew daily weaker; the warm
weather brought no relief, and the autumn was
unfavorable to her. Karl was frequently with
her, and other friends were assiduous in atten-
tions. Karl's daughter, staying with her, writes
to Fritz : "In the evening come at times visitors, who surround grandmother's easy chair,
and often when she does not understand she
gives a friendly nod. But to-day she lies in
bed. The crown-princess [Maria Paulowna]
comes to see grandmother every week. The
crown-prince, too, looks in daily to see how she
gets on."

To Goethe Charlotte sent felicitations on
his seventy-eighth birthday, August, 28, 1826.
In answer, he sent his poem addressed to the
friends who congratulated him on his jubilee,
and with it the following note, the last he
wrote to her: the first was written fifty years
before.

"WEIMAR, 29*th August*, 1826.

" The accompanying poem, my dearest, ought
properly to end as follows : ' But to see affec-

tion and love maintain themselves through so many, many years between near neighbors, is the highest that can be given to man.' And so forth and so forth."

On awaking one morning she said : " Every one has a trouble. I am very obliging, but these people have no money ; it will do no good." On being asked what she meant, she said : " Why, Schiller will have it that I shall collect subscriptions for him, but I don't know how to set about it ; I shall not succeed." When she perceived that she had been dreaming, she laughed heartily. At Christmas, 1826, she was so weak it was thought she would not survive the day ; but she rallied, and entered 1827 and her eighty-sixth year.

In the room adjoining hers were visitors and inquirers from morning till night. Karl writes to his brother Fritz : " Louischen [Karl's daughter] is now in attendance upon her. I cannot help much, but she thinks herself deserted when two or three of us are not with her. Stiefen [Charlotte's maid] has an endurance, patience, and activity such as I never witnessed before ; night and day she is on her feet."

Charlotte grew daily weaker, and prayed for release. On the fifth, in the evening, she lay in bed, free from pain. At seven, after bidding Karl good-night, she fell into a gentle sleep, from which she waked no more on earth, and at the same hour the next evening, the sixth of January, 1827, breathed her last. A few days before, she had given directions for her funeral, and requested that the procession should not pass under Goethe's windows, which was its natural course, for fear that the view of it might give him pain. Schiller was in her latest dreams, Goethe in her latest waking thoughts.

THE END.

www.ingramcontent.com/pod-product-compliance
Lightning Source LLC
Chambersburg PA
CBHW060605030726
47498CB00005B/1547